The Wish

The Wish

Gail Carson Levine

SCHOLASTIC INC.

New York Toronto London Auckland Sydney
Mexico City New Delhi Hong Kong

ISBN 0-439-29787-7

12 11 10 9 8 7 6   2 3 4 5 6/0

Printed in the U.S.A.   40

First Scholastic printing, September 2001

Typography by Michele N. Tupper

To Bunny Gabel

and her class of geniuses

—many thanks.

The Wish

Prologue

The old lady looked wobbly and feeble. The minute our subway train started, she was going to keel over. Then she'd be a sick passenger, and the train would stop while we waited for an ambulance, and I'd be late for school.

Plus she looked terrified. I gave her my seat. I helped her into it.

"Thank you, dear. You have done me a good turn." She didn't have an old lady's voice. Her tones were as round and juicy as an anchorwoman's. "And you know what they say about good turns—"

"That's okay." Was she going to tip me? "I don't want anything."

"Yes, you do, Wilma. You want many things. I will give you one."

How did she know my name?

The train stopped at Twenty-eighth Street. I thought

about going to another car, but I was getting off at the next stop.

"What is your wish?" she asked. The train started moving again. "I know whether you tell me or not. But you ought to put it positively."

The train stopped. We were between stations. In the silence, the old lady continued, "It should not be, 'I wish I weren't always left out or picked on.'"

She knew. And now so did everybody in our car. I looked around. Only adults, thank goodness. The train got going again.

"I can make your wish come true. You will be a sought-after member of the in crowd. You will be a cool cat."

The train screeched into the Twenty-third Street station. My stop.

The doors opened. I stood half in, half out, keeping them open. I didn't want to be just a member of the in crowd. I wanted more. "I want to be the *most* popular kid at Claverford," I blurted out. I figured I might as well go all the way with a wish nobody could grant.

She frowned. "Is it wise . . . ? All right, dear. Granted."

Chapter One

I once read that in some primitive tribe or other, they punished people by ignoring them. If you were being punished, nobody would talk to you. They'd look through you, they'd pretend you didn't exist. It wouldn't take long for this treatment to kill you. I mean, you'd actually die. Dead.

I didn't die, but for the first nine months of eighth grade I almost wished I had. Before then, I had not one but two best friends, Tracy and Freda. We'd been friends since kindergarten. But then Tracy moved to Connecticut, and Freda's parents got mad at Claverford. They said the teachers weren't developmentally aware enough. They sent Freda to a boarding school even though we had only one more year to go before high school.

At first I wasn't worried. I figured I'd make more friends at school. But it turned out making new friends wasn't easy—or even possible. Cliques had already been established, and I couldn't break in. Or maybe I didn't have the knack of showing people that I was okay. Fun. Nice, even.

At first, the other kids weren't out-and-out mean. They let me sit with them at lunch—but nobody talked to me. If I had to call somebody about homework, whoever it was would answer my questions—the same way you take messages for your parents—bored, but vaguely polite.

Then, in November, it got worse. Much worse. Ms. Hannah, my teacher for homeroom and language arts, told us to write two pages on our "secret lives."

"This is the creative in creative writing, children." Ms. Hannah was the only teacher who still called us "children." She also pronounced "blue" as b-l-y-e-w.

I wrote seven pages pretending to be my Airedale, Reggie. I could have written a hundred pages. I love animals, I love dogs, and I especially love Reggie.

I wrote about dog happiness, about what dog dreams were like, about how it felt to chase a squirrel, about my favorite flavor of dog biscuit, and about my feud with the German shepherd who lived across the hall. But that's not what got me in trouble when Ms. Hannah read my report out loud.

She started out by saying she wanted us to hear the

best example of "point of view" she'd ever come across in a student's writing. I relaxed in my chair, waiting to hear yet another piece by Daphne, who was adored by Ms. Hannah and avoided by everyone on our side of the teacher's desk.

"Wilma is to be congratulated on her exemplary effort, which you shall now hear."

I wished I could vaporize and reassemble in a middle school in Moscow. If I had thought anyone else would hear my paper, I would have written the kind of thing everybody else wrote, like my secret life as a music video star, or my secret life as a pro basketball player.

The awful part began halfway down the first page, when Ms. Hannah read, "'I hear the elevator door open. It is my beloved Wilma coming home from school.'" And then—even worse—"'My beloved Wilma is asleep. From the foot of the bed, I watch her. She is so beautiful.'"

Everybody was laughing so hard that Ms. Hannah had to wait five minutes before she could continue. Was she going to read all seven pages? I could survive what she'd read so far, but not if she kept going.

She kept going. "'I see Celeste, the dalmatian who is my best friend after my beloved Wilma. She is peeing. I rush to smell her pee. Celeste had chicken for dinner. I lift my leg over her pee.'"

The class howled. Timothy stamped his feet. BeeBee moaned that *she* had to pee. They all looked at me and looked away again laughing harder than ever. It took Ms. Hannah five more minutes to get them to quiet down. I wished they never would. I knew what came next.

"'Then I sniff her anus. It smells rich and full of Celeste.'"

After that, Ms. Hannah lost control of the class.

From that day on nobody talked to me, except for the occasional woof or snuffling noise as I walked through the halls—and that wasn't conversation. I was left strictly alone, with only three exceptions.

The first exception was Jared, who sat next to me in language arts. He told me he liked my secret life. He said it made him understand dogs better than he had before. I was glad to hear it, but I wasn't interested in Jared Fein, whose eyebrows met over his nose, forming one long continuous eyebrow.

The second exception was Ardis Lundy, the most popular girl at Claverford. She had Ms. Hannah for sixth period, and Ms. Hannah had been kind enough to read my secret life there, too.

"I'm glad she didn't read mine," Ardis told me. "I pretended I was my grandmother, raising my mother. It was pretty personal." And she smiled at me.

After that, she'd smile and wave when she saw me, but then again, she smiled and waved to everybody.

The third exception was Suzanne Russo. Razor Mouth Suzanne Russo. From then on she'd call me "beloved Wilma," or ask me what I'd sniffed lately or if there were any good fire hydrants near school. And no matter what else she said, she'd always drag the word "anus" in somehow.

Then, two weeks after The Reading, I got a lucky break. Mr. Pashkin, our communications teacher, paired everyone off for debates, and he paired me with BeeBee Molzen, who was very popular. Our topic was human cloning, and we were supposed to work together on our arguments before we debated in front of everybody. I thought this could be my chance to make a new friend, and then to make even more friends if BeeBee brought me into her clique.

That afternoon BeeBee and I met after school at the public library. And we had fun. I told her I didn't like public speaking, and she said she always lost debates, even with her little brother. I predicted I'd make great arguments in a whisper nobody could hear, and she predicted she'd just say, "Duh, uh, clone, uh, duh."

I took the side that cloning humans was ethical, and BeeBee took the opposite side. I helped her look up arguments against me, and she gave me tips to get rid of stage fright. Then we agreed to meet again at the library the next day to practice and do more research.

I thought we had made progress in becoming friends. I hadn't made an idiot of myself; I'd even made her laugh a few times. But when I asked her if she wanted to walk over together, she said she couldn't. She said she'd meet me there because she had to talk to her friends first.

I knew I had a way to go.

The next day, after we finished preparing for the debate, we talked about what it would be like to have clones of ourselves. BeeBee, who liked to paint, said she wouldn't need a mirror to do a self-portrait. I said I'd like enough clones to gang up on my older sister, Maud.

"And if there were a clone of me," I added, "she'd be younger, and I'd have a little sister."

"I wish I had a little sister too," BeeBee said. "But they wouldn't clone a dope like me."

"They wouldn't clone me either," I said. (Secretly I thought they might, though, after I made history in veterinary medicine.)

And then BeeBee said sure they'd clone me, and I said she wasn't a dope, and I really thought we had taken a few steps toward being friends. The day after that, the seat next to her at lunch was empty. I gathered my courage and said, "Can I sit here?" I could swear the whole cafeteria fell silent at just that second.

BeeBee never looked up and never said anything. Evadney Jones, president of SGO, our student government organization, said they were holding the chair for somebody who was coming in a minute. When I turned away, I heard giggles.

And that was that. Except I did extra research for our debate and worked out more arguments on my side. And when we debated, I didn't just win, I demolished BeeBee. I made her look stupid. And afterward I felt only the tiniest bit bad for her. Hardly bad at all.

I stopped trying to make friends after that. I just went through the day trying to ignore everyone, except they ignored me first, and better.

I solved the problem of where to sit at lunch by bringing sandwiches from home. I ate them in the girls' bathroom on the fourth floor, as far away from the cafeteria as possible. It was a disgusting place to eat, but in the bathroom I didn't feel so alone because I wasn't in the middle of everybody else having people to talk to.

There were other loners at school, of course—Daphne, Jared, a kid named Benjy, and a few more. You'd think I could have made friends with one of them,

Daphne maybe, or she could have made friends with me. But it didn't work that way. She didn't try to be my friend and I didn't try to be hers.

I saw the other loners the way everyone else did—as unappealing, as to be avoided at all costs. If I hung out with one of them, I thought, my unpopular status would get worse, not better, because it would be magnified by association. I thought I'd lose any chance of changing things.

Not admirable, I guess—but true. Probably true for Daphne. Definitely true for me.

Anyway, day after day, I became so used to swallowing around a lump in my throat that when I caught strep throat in February, I didn't realize I was sick. I just thought the lump had gotten bigger. Mom noticed I was sick, though, and I had to stay home for two wonderful weeks. I had a high fever, and it felt like a knife was stuck in my throat, and I was deliriously happy.

Chapter Two

After my strep throat, I wanted to get the flu, mono, a broken leg—anything that wasn't terminal or disfiguring. But I stayed healthy.

When I went back to school, nothing changed. And nothing had changed three months later when I met the old lady on the subway. I didn't expect her to make any difference either, and she didn't. On the subway stairs I was surrounded by laughing, yelling kids, but I was alone. The usual.

Outside, it had just stopped raining, and the breeze was chilly. I was cold, even though it was May twenty-sixth.

The old lady must have guessed about my wanting to be popular, I reasoned. Most kids want that. Though how she knew my name was a mystery. Nobody names a kid Wilma. The last person before me to be named Wilma was prehistoric—a Flintstone.

Maybe I look like a Wilma. My neck is short, and my front teeth are long, like a beaver. Everything else about me is average, although my brown eyes add to the beaver look. A friendly beaver, that's me.

At the corner of West Twenty-fourth and Tenth, I saw Ardis half a block behind me with a few billion of her friends. Even though she had talked to me on the "beloved Wilma" day, she hardly knew me. Claverford is small enough for everybody to know everybody, but I knew her better than she knew me. It's like you know things about the President of the United States, but he—or she—doesn't know you from a lima bean.

Ordinarily, I would have kept on walking. But this morning, because I was cold, and tired of being invisible and alone, and because of the old lady, I decided to talk to Ardis. I waited at the curb for her.

One of the bunch with Ardis was Razor Mouth Suzanne. Suzanne had always clung by her fingernails to the popular clique. She lived in the same building as me, and I'd known her since we were five, when she decapitated a snowman I was making.

Suzanne was tiny and perfect and had a teeny voice that carried a million miles. She reminded me of a Pomeranian—fox face and needle-sharp bark, and nervous, darting brown eyes.

Ardis, on the other hand, was tall and big boned and regal. She was African American, with the shaggy hair of an Irish water spaniel. Her nose was hawkish, but her eyes were huge and an amazing blue-gray, and her mouth was made for lipstick ads.

The group was getting closer. What could I say to Ardis? I thought of possible topics of conversation. She was on the track team and in the debating club. In the fall, she'd been elected to SGO, but I'd once overheard Suzanne telling somebody that Ardis was failing half her subjects and might get kicked out.

"Hi, Ardis," I said.

"Wilma—beloved!" Suzanne yelped.

Somebody giggled. I heard a low "woof."

Suzanne went on. "Sniffed any yummy—"

Ardis interrupted her. "Hi, Wilma." She smiled at me.

She was so nice.

"Hi," I said.

"How're you doing?" It wasn't really a question, and she didn't wait for an answer. She started to cross the street with her friends.

But I pretended she did want to know. "I'm okay," I said. So far, so good. Now what else could I say? I stood on the curb, thinking. If she was failing half her subjects, maybe I could say something to help. I called after her, "If you want, I could help you out in science and history." My best subjects.

She turned and yelled at me while walking backward across the street. She wasn't smiling anymore. "Who says I need help? The last thing I need is—"

A truck drove between us and drowned her out. It was near my side of the street, and it plowed through a puddle, drenching me from my waist to my feet.

When the truck had passed, Ardis and her friends were way down the block. I was soaked and cold and dirty. That was so dumb of me, to remind Ardis of her bad grades. How could I possibly have thought it would make her like me?

And now I'd given Suzanne something new to laugh at me about.

Some help the old lady had been. If she hadn't tottered into my life, I wouldn't have waited for Ardis. And if I hadn't waited, I'd be dry and unpopular right now, which would be an improvement.

I stood there, hating to show up at school looking this way.

There's Wilma. She splashed through a puddle to chase a stick.

There's Wilma. Another dog peed on her.

There's Wilma. Gross.

I started squelching to school. At least I didn't have far to go. Claverford was straight ahead, on the northeast corner of Eleventh Avenue and Twenty-fourth Street. It stood out on a block of shoe-box factory buildings because of its zany architecture, which it was famous for. It looked like it had been assembled by a goofy giant playing with blocks. The small blocks were classrooms. The big ones were the auditorium, the cafeteria, and the library.

It was also famous for being the richest middle school in the country. If you went there, either you were smart and had a scholarship, or your parents were loaded. In spite of our ugly uniforms, which were supposed to make it impossible to tell, everybody knew who was a Brain and who was a Wallet.

Suzanne and I were Brains, although in her case I think they made a mistake. Ardis was a smart Wallet. You couldn't be a dope and survive in the debating club.

Some of the most popular kids were Brains and some were Wallets. Money didn't matter. Beauty didn't either. For example, everybody liked BeeBee, my debate opponent, even though she had no chin and almost no forehead. And her boyfriend was Carlos the Adorable, the same Carlos I'd had a crush on for the last two years.

The crowd of kids grew denser as I approached the

school's tall wooden doors. Two girls jostled me, and neither one apologized. A four-hundred-pound hiking boot squashed my foot. We weren't supposed to wear hiking boots to school.

I limped under the overhang and took a few steps into the building.

Ardis and some of her friends stood under the clock in the lobby. "Hey, Wilma." She waved and moved toward me, and her group moved with her.

"You're wet." She smiled at me. "A bus splashed me last week. It was terrible. I was soaked and muddy for hours."

"Wilma . . ." Suzanne began.

She was going to ask if a hydrant had opened on me. Or something nastier.

". . . I never noticed your eyelashes before. They're gorgeous." Suzanne looked around at everybody. "Aren't they?"

They all nodded and looked friendly.

Huh?

Chapter Three

"I have to dry off," I said.

Ardis and Suzanne followed me into the bathroom. I pulled a wad of paper towels out of the dispenser and dabbed at my wet skirt. Suzanne took some paper towels too and tried to help me.

Ardis leaned against a sink. "Suzanne says you're her best friend."

Was something wrong with my hearing?

"She is," Suzanne said. "We live in the same building. We've been friends practically since we were born."

"We're just neighbors."

"Where do you live?" Ardis asked.

"On Sixty-sixth. The big building on—"

"You know where we live," Suzanne said. "I invited you to my birthday party. Remember? The address was on the invitation. Only you couldn't make it."

Her best friend—me—hadn't even known there was a party.

"Where do you live?" I asked Ardis.

"On Irving Place." She paused. "Look, if you meant it before, I could use some help with history. Maybe you can come over sometime and we can study together."

The truck had run me over instead of just splashing me. I was dead and this was Hell and Heaven rolled into one. Suzanne and Ardis for friends.

"How come you're talking to me? What's going on?" Since I was dead, it was safe to say whatever I wanted.

Ardis looked puzzled. "I like you." Her face went blank for a second. "I don't know why."

"Why shouldn't we talk to you?" Suzanne asked. "You're the most popular kid at Claverford."

The old lady! The old lady?

☼ ☼ ☼

The hallucination continued. I left Ardis to go to language arts, where my humiliation by Ms. Hannah had taken place.

When I got there, Erica was trying to yank Daphne

out of the seat to the left of mine. I usually sat between Jared and Daphne, the other two loners. But today Carlos was in the chair to the right of mine. Timothy was in my chair. Everybody else was standing.

As soon as he saw me, Timothy patted his legs. "Special cushion, Wilma. Park it here."

This wasn't happening.

BeeBee said, "You're too bony. She'll be disabled for life."

Timothy didn't get up, so I sat near the back, next to the windows. As soon as I did, there was a scramble, like in musical chairs. Evadney Jones, president of SGO, wound up sprawled on the floor at my feet. Suzanne got the chair next to me. Trust her to get what she wanted. BeeBee was in front of me, and Jared was behind. Timothy hopped around, yowling, "Who stepped on me?"

Ms. Hannah arrived. "What on earth? I want all of you to go to your seats."

Evadney stood and dusted herself off. Timothy limped away. "Offer stands, Wilma. Anytime."

I went to my regular seat. Jared sat down next to me, grinning like he'd won the lottery.

"Now before you pass in your reports," Ms. Hannah

said, "I should like some of you to tell us about the marvelous books you read."

No hands went up.

"Daphne, you may start."

Daphne, Brain and class valedictorian, was Ms. Hannah's favorite.

"I enjoyed *The Joy Luck Club* because it has folk stories, which were new to me since they're Chinese—"

"And you're Martian."

"That's sufficient, Timothy. You may take a turn, after Daphne, since you're in a talkative frame of mind."

I didn't hear either of their reports. Camilla, who sat behind me, passed me a note. It had my name on the outside. Daphne passed me a note. Jared handed me two more. I looked around the room. Everybody was writing or folding pieces of paper.

If Ms. Hannah had seen the notes, she might have been happy, because a lot of creative writing was going on. But she had started talking about "*Hamlet* by the bard," and she didn't notice anything.

Some of the notes were signed and some weren't. Daphne, Evadney, and Nina each asked me to sit with them at lunch. Daphne promised me her slice of chocolate mousse cake if I did. Evadney wrote that she'd tell me something she'd never told anyone else before. Nina offered to share food and tales of love and life at Claverford.

Somebody (unsigned note) asked if I wanted to go to the Central Park Zoo on Sunday. The zoo was my favorite place, but how was I supposed to answer if I didn't know who was asking me?

Two notes were poems. One said,

> *Wilma's sweet.*
> *She's a treat.*
> *Let's make a date.*
> *We'll call it fate.*
> *Boo hoo.*
> *I love you.*

Definitely a Wallet.
The other one was from a Brain.

> *My barking siren*
> *My short-necked beauty*
> *My long-toothed divine*
> *Tie me to a tall mast*

So I may not come at you
Stop my mouth with a silk bandanna
That I may not tell my hope
I think and dream and drink of you

If this was death, who needed life?

Chapter Four

By the end of last period, I had collected over a hundred notes. Forty were from boys who wanted me to go to Grad Night with them—but only eighteen were signed. Grad Night was Claverford's version of a senior prom, except Grad Night happened the Friday before graduation, which was just three weeks away.

Forty boys! Half the boys in our grade wanted me— me!—for their Grad Night date. Four of the signed notes were from boys who already had girlfriends, including my secret love, Carlos, who was going with BeeBee.

Carlos kept trying to catch my eye during language arts. He'd never paid any attention to me before. This had been quite a feat for him one time last year, when we had been stuck alone together in the school elevator for ten minutes. I had talked to him, of course, since it was my big chance to make him know me, care for me.

But he had managed not even to glance my way, and not to say more than, "Uhhh . . ."

I wondered if Carlos was the one who'd asked me to go to the zoo.

If my wish had really come true, it was almost worth the last nine months of misery. I wasn't ignored or teased once all day. The word "anus" wasn't ever mentioned. If I died, almost five hundred kids would go to my funeral, and the school would have to bring in extra grief counselors to comfort everybody.

But how could my wish have come true? It didn't seem reasonable that all my problems could be over simply because I had given an old lady my seat, especially since I'd done it partly so I wouldn't be late for school.

And if it had come true, if it was a spell, how was I different from before? I didn't feel different. When I looked at myself in the bathroom mirror, I didn't look different. I was acting like myself. But nobody was seeing the same Wilma they had seen yesterday.

So assuming it *was* a spell, how long would the old lady's gratitude last? Would I still be popular tomorrow, and if I was, for how long after that? Would it still be with me next year at Elliot, the high school most Claverford kids went to? Would it last me through college? For the rest of my life? Or would it end in the next five minutes?

And if it ended, how would I stand it?

※　※　※

Ardis and Suzanne were waiting for me in the lobby when school was over. Let me repeat that—*Ardis* was waiting for *me*. Suzanne saw me first. Her popularity radar was infallible.

"Wilma. Over here."

I threaded my way through the crowd, smiling and saying "hi" to everybody. I reached Ardis. "Hi," I said to her. I ignored Suzanne.

"What's happening, Wilma?" Ardis asked.

I don't think I'd ever grinned before the way I did then. Ardis got the full power of the day I'd had. "I don't know what's happening. But whatever it is, it's fabulous."

She smiled back at me. "Way to go."

She walked me to the subway, along with Suzanne and at least twenty other kids. Ardis didn't say anything, just walked next to me.

"Do you have any pets?" I asked. It was the first thing I wanted to know about anybody, though, given my reputation, maybe I shouldn't have brought up the subject.

She shook her head.

Oh. That was a disappointment.

"Me neither," Suzanne said.

"I have Shanara, my little sister." Ardis laughed. She had the best laugh—genuine and shoulder shaking. A whole body laugh, not a brain laugh, and nothing mean about it. "Shanara follows me around like a dog. She's eight, and she's sweet."

Suzanne said, "I'm an only ch—"

"My sister Maud is four years older than me," I said. "If she ever called me sweet, I'd faint."

I didn't know what to say next, but Ardis asked which teachers I had. We compared while Suzanne kept interrupting with the teachers she had. Ardis had Mr. Pike for science, and I'd had him in seventh grade. He was good for months of conversation—how he picked his ears with a bent paper clip; how his Adam's apple was so big, it looked like he'd swallowed a golf ball; how he rocked back and forth till you almost got seasick.

I told her about the time last year when he gave us a test, and he started rocking, and he rocked so hard, he fell off his chair.

She laughed again. I had made Ardis Lundy laugh. Twice. Me.

Mr. Pike lasted us to the subway. Ardis didn't take

the subway to get home, so we said good-bye, and I was left with Suzanne. I wished she had gone too.

"I always wanted a dog," Suzanne told me while we waited for our train.

"So you could write a secret-life essay like I did?"

"Yeah. That was a super essay. So imaginative."

I pinched myself. It hurt.

Our train came. "I thought I'd look cute walking a tiny poodle," Suzanne continued as we got on, "but Daddy said I'd have to pick up after it, and that's disgusting."

If you love an animal, you don't mind what goes along with it.

"Guess what." Suzanne smiled. Smirked, really.

"What?"

"I have history with Ardis. I saw the last test Bluestein gave back to her. She got a fifty-seven."

Suzanne being friendly was as mean as Suzanne being mean.

"So she failed one test," I said.

The train stopped at our station, Sixty-sixth Street. Suzanne gossiped all the way home. She told me that Evadney Jones's friends had cheated when they had counted the votes for SGO president. She said that Erica couldn't afford to go to Elliot next year because her mother had lost her job.

We went into our building. My apartment was on the third floor, and Suzanne's was on eighteen. She rang for the elevator and I headed for the stairs. I just couldn't stand to spend another second with her.

"Want to come up and hang out?" she asked.

"No." I knew I was being rude, but I didn't care.

"Okay." She punched the elevator button again. "I ought to study too."

Now I felt guilty. Guilty enough to say, "See you tomorrow." But not guilty enough to change my mind.

The phone was ringing as I unlocked our door. While Reggie jumped all over me, Maud yelled, "It's for you, Wilma."

How could she tell the phone was for me when it was still ringing? We didn't have caller ID. We didn't even have an answering machine.

It was BeeBee. I could hardly hear her over Reggie's enthusiastic barking.

"What?" I shouted.

I clamped the phone between my head and my shoulder and stroked Reggie with both hands, which got him quiet enough for me to hear that she was inviting me to her house for a sleepover Friday night. I thought of turning her down because of the way she had acted when we were working on the debate. But then she said

Ardis and Nina Draper were coming too, and I decided to forgive her.

The three most popular kids at school.

And me.

Wow.

Chapter Five

After I hung up, I went on petting Reggie. The sleep-over would be incredible. I'd have fun. I'd be on the inside for a change. Anything could happen.

The phone rang again. It was Jared Fein. One-eyebrow Jared.

"I only have a minute," I said. "I have to walk my dog." A lie. Maud did the afternoon walk.

Silence on the line.

"Look, I have to go," I said.

"Wait. Uh, I wrote the note about going to the zoo."

Just my luck.

"Wilma? Are you there?"

"Yeah."

"Do you want to go?"

Not with him. "I can't." Why not? I had to say a reason. "I have to study for the language arts final."

"Oh." He sounded disappointed. Which was nice.

"What are you working on?"

"*Hamlet*." I imitated Ms. Hannah's deep, over-dramatic voice. "'By the bard.'"

"I like *Hamlet*. 'This above all—to thine own self be true. . . .' What if we study together at the zoo?"

I was trapped. It was too late to say I was having brain surgery to make me think up better excuses.

"Okay," I said. Anyway, it would be my first date. That was something. "I'll come. I love the zoo."

After I hung up, Maud came out of our room, holding a notebook.

We share a bedroom. She complains that it's not fair for a person of her maturity, which she says is far beyond mine, to have to room with a child veterinarian. I point out that it's not fair to me either. If I had my own room, I'd have more than just a dog. I'd have hamsters and a rabbit. For starters. Mom says life isn't fair, and if she ever gets rich, she'll buy a mansion with a wing for each of us.

"Are you okay? Did something bad happen today?" Maud actually sounded pleasant. Was I popular with her now too?

"I'm all right. Why?"

"You're sure? The phone hasn't stopped ringing since I got back from walking the dog." She always called

Reggie "the dog." "All these kids phoned." She tore the back page out of her notebook. "There were more, but they didn't leave their names."

I took the page. Kids I'd never talked to had called me. "I'm fine. Really."

"Oh. Good. Then I'm telling Mom that I'm not your answering service. I have a pa—"

The phone rang. I answered it, and Maud went back into our room and slammed the door.

It was Ardis. "BeeBee says you're coming Friday. That's great."

"I can't wait."

Silence. If she had nothing to say, she said nothing.

But I wanted to keep the conversation going. "Um," I said. I didn't want to talk about my subway ride home with Suzanne, and going to the zoo with Jared was nothing to boast about. "Are you studying?"

"Yeah. I have a Russian test tomorrow."

Suzanne had to be wrong. They didn't let you take Russian unless your grades were good.

"Can you read the alphabet?"

"Cyrillic? Sure. It's not as bad as Chinese."

"Are you studying Chinese?" They didn't give it at Claverford.

"No. Someday maybe."

"Oh. I'm taking French."

"Ooh la la."

"Ms. Osnoe says that all the time. She says . . ."

We were talking about teachers again, but I couldn't think of another topic.

After we hung up, there were six more calls before Mom got home. Except for a telemarketer, they were all for me. One was from Carlos.

"You looked good today," he said.

"Thanks. You looked handsome." Did I really say that?

"Uhhhh. Uhhh. Thanks. Uhhh. Do you want to hang out together after school tomorrow?"

"What about BeeBee?"

"What about her?"

I had just accepted an invitation to BeeBee's sleepover. I couldn't take her boyfriend away from her. Even though I *could*. But maybe that wasn't what he had in mind.

"Will she be there?"

"I doubt it."

"I can't make it. I have to go home."

"That's cool," he said. "Well, 'bye."

Reggie rushed to the door, wagging his tail wildly. It had to be Mom. Then I heard her key in the lock.

We always ate right after Mom came home. She was the dietitian at a school for developmentally disabled children. Most nights she brought our dinner home with her, whatever the residents had eaten. It was a perk. We'd never starve, even though she didn't make much money and Dad didn't have much to send either.

As I was putting our plates on the table, the phone rang again. Maud, who was waiting for food to be dropped in front of her, told Mom it was for me.

"How do you know . . ." Mom answered it. "I'm sorry. You'll have to call Wilma back. We're having dinner."

As soon as she hung up, the phone rang again. Mom looked at me. Before today, almost nobody had called me for nine long months.

"This has been going on all afternoon," Maud said.

"What's up, Wilma?" Mom asked after she turned off the phone without answering it.

I shrugged, but she just waited.

"Well . . ." What could I say? "Um . . . one of the most popular girls decided she likes me, and now everybody does. I guess I'm a fad."

"Eighth grade!" Maud snorted. "I'd die if I had to do it over."

The next morning everybody was glad to see me again. When I got on my train, two Claverford kids were already there, and they called me over. When we got out of the subway, more and more kids kept joining us, all of them maneuvering to be close to me.

If you did this, old lady, thank you. Thank you.

On the way to school, during school, and after school, kids kept asking me about Reggie. I guess the only thing they knew about me was that I had a dog. Camilla wanted to know his age. Erica asked if he could do tricks. Daphne showed me a picture of her sheepdog.

Evadney was the first to go beyond animals. She asked if I had any brothers or sisters. Soon they'd be asking about my choice of shampoo and whether my favorite snack was pretzels or popcorn.

❂ ❂ ❂

After school on Friday I had to go home and walk Reggie, since Maud would do the morning walk for me on Saturday while I was at BeeBee's.

All I could think about while I walked him was the sleepover. I would get to know Ardis and BeeBee and

Nina better, especially Ardis. I'd try to figure out what made them popular. Then, if the spell ended, I'd know how to act to keep having my wish.

But what if it ended while I was there? What if we were all sitting around talking and it ended, and they went back to seeing me as the old me? But I *was* the old me; I hadn't changed. They were the ones who were different.

I tried to remember my exact conversation with the old lady. I remembered that she had offered to make me part of the in crowd. And I had said I wanted to be the most popular kid at Claverford. Then she had said something else. What was it? She asked if it was wise. What could she have meant by that? Where else would I want to be popular but at school?

After Reggie's walk, I checked myself in the mirror. I was wearing jeans and a T-shirt with an Airedale's face printed on it. I got my backpack, slung it over my shoulder, and went back to the mirror. I looked cool.

As I was leaving, Reggie bounded to the door, ready for another walk. I knelt and held his head in my hands. "I'll miss you, Reggie-weggie." I stroked his ears, and he licked my chin. "I have to go, boy."

He caught on that I was going without him, and his tail went down to its position of absolute misery.

"Don't you want me to have human friends too?" I went to the biscuit stash in the cabinet under the sink. A consolation prize for him.

He wouldn't take it. His eyes said, "Biscuits are nothing compared to the pleasure of your company."

"It's just one night," I pleaded.

Reggie's eyes answered, "How do I know you will come back?"

I was getting exasperated. "I go to school every day."

"I'm used to that," his eyes said. "But this is desertion, abandonment."

What if I took him with me? He'd be something to talk about. I knew I should check first, but then I decided to take a chance. As long as the spell held, they couldn't hate me for it. Mom wasn't home yet, so I yelled to Maud that I was leaving. She came out of her room.

"I'm not taking phone messages for you," she said. "I'm not a secretary."

"Just tell my fans that Reggie and I are on safari, and we—"

"You're taking Reggie to a sleepover? Bad move."

Not for me. I was popular!

Chapter Six

If I hadn't had Reggie, I would have taken the bus to BeeBee's. This way, it was a long walk. But when we arrived, I was glad he was there. BeeBee was a Wallet, and I would have felt uncomfortable walking up to her doorman without purebred Reggie at the end of a leash.

Her apartment was on the top floor, the thirty-fourth. I made Reggie sit while I rang the bell.

The three of them—Ardis, Nina, and BeeBee—answered the door. I was wearing the wrong clothes. They were in shorts and cotton shirts. Worse, BeeBee and Nina looked like they'd never seen a dog before. Ardis's head was down, so I couldn't see her face. It was the end of my popularity. I'd blown it with Reggie.

But then BeeBee squatted in front of him. "What a sweet baby. What a good boy. I love you too." She scratched under Reggie's chin and behind his ears. He tried to lick her face, and his tail wagged frantically.

"This may be the first time a dog came to a sleep-over," Nina said.

"Hear that, Reggie? You're making history." I grinned at Nina.

She didn't smile back. "It's pretty weird, Wilma. Five points off for strange behavior."

Had the spell ended?

BeeBee said, "That's Nina's way of saying she's glad you're here."

"Is it okay, BeeBee?" I asked. "Do you mind, Nina? Ardis?"

Ardis wasn't there. She must have gone back into the apartment.

"My brother's allergic to dogs," BeeBee said. "Of course, he won't be in the room with us . . ."

"Should I take him home?"

"Would you come back?"

This was great! "Sure I'd come back. It's just that Reggie didn't want me to leave before."

"Oh . . . let's try it. Mom can't kill me. Right? Besides, nobody has to know."

How could they not know? Our apartment was so small you couldn't bring in a caterpillar undetected.

She went on. "Dad said we could sleep upstairs in

his studio. Hold the pooch." She led me in.

I stepped into a small circular vestibule with doors to the left and right and a spiral staircase straight ahead. Reggie's toenails sounded like a hailstorm as he rushed across.

There was no door at the top of the stairs, just space—a loft as big and almost as tall as the auditorium at school, with floor-to-ceiling windows all the way around.

I let go of Reggie. We were in a forest of sculptures. They were elongated stick figures made of metal. The arms and legs were long cylinders. The heads were ovals with triangles for noses. The figures were about sixteen feet tall, and they were in athletic poses—stretching, bending, standing on one foot with the other leg high in the air.

"Your dad is a sculptor," I said idiotically.

"He says he was Degas in a previous life."

"BeeBee paints," Nina said. "She's very talented."

"I'm a colorist," BeeBee said, "and I use a lot of impasto."

Whatever that was. I nodded enthusiastically.

"Show her—"

"Wiiilmaaa!"

It was a strangled scream, coming from the other end of the room. Ardis was pressed into a corner, hands over her head, while Reggie wagged his tail and sniffed her crotch.

"Get it away from me. Hurry, before I—"

"Come, Reggie." He came. "What a good boy! What a good doggie!" I scratched his back. "You train a dog by telling him he's a hero when he does something right. They like praise better than dog biscuits."

"So do I," Nina said.

BeeBee and I laughed.

"I can't stay," Ardis said, walking toward us. "I just remembered. My sister's in a play at her school, and I promised to go."

"You're afraid of dogs." As soon as the words came out of my mouth, I knew I shouldn't have said them.

"You don't know me," Ardis said, mad. "You have no idea what I'm afraid of and what I'm not afraid of." Then she calmed down and sort of smiled. "And I'm really afraid of what Shanara will do to me if I miss her play."

She was leaving because of Reggie, and she was the main reason I wanted to come in the first place.

"Can't you call her?" BeeBee said. "You could say I'm going through an emo—"

"Reggie won't—Reggie?" I said. I looked around for him.

There he was, halfway across the room, sniffing around the statues. He was especially interested in one.

"No, Reggie! No!"

I was too late. He had lifted his leg on one of the stretching figures. Pee was running down the metal.

Chapter Seven

"Bad Reggie! Bad boy! He never goes indoors. I'll clean it up. I'm sorry." What would happen now? Would they throw me out? Would they hate me?

"Dad'll kill me! The patina on the metal is real important to him."

"I'll clean it up."

"We'll clean it up," Nina said. "I think you should take Reggie home right now, Wilma."

"She's right," BeeBee said.

They were throwing me out. I put on Reggie's leash and started down the stairs. Why did I have to bring him? Why did I have to push my popularity?

"Hurry back," Ardis called.

"Right!" BeeBee added. "We're going to eat soon."

They wanted me to come back! And Ardis would still be here! I was invincible!

After I dropped Reggie off and ignored Maud's "I

told you so," I waited on Sixty-fifth Street for the bus. While I stood there, Daphne rounded the corner. I looked the other way, but she saw me.

"Hi," she said.

I may have been unpopular this year, but Daphne may never have had a friend in her life. She was as pale and limp as cooked spaghetti, with a voice to match.

"You're waiting for the bus?" she asked.

I nodded. I wished it would come.

"That was dumb of me," she said. "What else could you be doing?"

I didn't say anything.

"You think I'm an idiot," she said.

Maybe. "No. I could be standing here for lots of reasons."

"Where are you going?"

The bus was half a block away. I didn't want her to feel bad because nobody had invited her to a sleepover. "Uhh . . ." There was an eyeglass store on the corner. "To the eye doctor." The bus pulled up. "See you."

She waved.

On the bus I decided there had been no reason for me to protect Daphne's feelings. Plenty of kids went to sleepovers. It was a fact of life. A fact of my life now. I had to toughen up.

When I got back to BeeBee's, it was seven thirty and Ardis was still there. Everybody was sitting on the floor, leaning against rolled-up sleeping bags and eating Chinese takeout.

The first thing I did was look at the spot where Reggie had peed. I couldn't tell. There was no stain, no holes in the metal. "It doesn't show," I said.

"It better not," Ardis said. "After all we did."

BeeBee nodded. "We used soap and detergent and disinfectant—everything except toothpaste. Then Nina did a curing spell, and we all felt better."

I guess I looked confused, because Nina said, "I'm very New Age. Points off for being out of it, Wilma."

I nodded like I understood.

"The chicken with cashews is good," Ardis said.

"Try the Szechuan shrimp," Nina said, pointing at the container with her chopsticks. "I like to chew on the red peppers and watch flames shoot out of my nose."

I sat between BeeBee and Ardis. Whenever I tried to use chopsticks, I wound up with food in my lap, so I took one of the plastic forks from the restaurant. But I felt uncomfortable eating differently from everyone else.

"Forks are much easier," Ardis said. "I don't know

why we bother with chopsticks." She reached for a fork.

I smiled at her. Ardis made you feel comfortable. Maybe that was her secret.

Then I had an amazing thought—did she switch so she could eat the way I did?

"We use chopsticks for the authentic Chinese experience," Nina said. "On a floor in a sculpture studio in Manhattan." She took a fork too. I couldn't believe it.

Downstairs, high heels clicked across the vestibule. A woman's voice rose from the stairwell. "I'm coming up."

BeeBee, Nina, and Ardis mouthed Mrs. Molzen's next words while she said them.

"Hide the contraband, girls. Here comes the fuzz."

"Hi, Mrs. Molzen," Ardis said.

"Greetings, Ardis, Nina." She stopped when she came to me.

"Mom, this is Wilma Sturtz."

I put my plate on the floor and stood up. "Hello, Mrs. Molzen."

She surveyed me. "Polite. The last time somebody stood—"

"Mom . . ." BeeBee said warningly.

"All right. No old-fogey talk. I just came up to see if you girls are having fun. Bernice Beryl, be sure to bring down the leftovers and the trash."

Bernice Beryl was BeeBee's real name? Astounding.

"Right, Mom."

Mrs. Molzen clattered back downstairs.

"Now you know the truth about me," BeeBee said. "My true name and my embarrassment of a mother."

"You should see my mother," I said. Then I felt disloyal. There was nothing wrong with Mom, except that she only let me have one dog and she made me share a room with Maud. "Your mom is fine," I added. "And so is mine."

"Do we have to talk about parents?" Nina said.

"What do you want to talk about?" Ardis asked.

"I don't know." Nina didn't say anything for a minute, and then she started listing other things she didn't want to talk about, like school, boys, and clothes.

Ardis giggled. "And let's not talk about presidential politics either."

I said, "Or least favorite vegetables."

They thought that was hysterical, and everybody started laughing, and I felt so great I could have floated up to the ceiling. Then we all started naming stupid topics, like shoe sizes and eyeglass prescriptions and names of insects. After that finally ran out, we were all quiet, in a good way, a wonderful way.

Finally Ardis said, "Turn out the lights, BeeBee. Show Wilma."

"Wait till you see." BeeBee walked to the hallway at the end of the loft.

She turned off the lights, and the room went dark. And New York City came inside with us. To the east and south, the buildings zoomed up, darker than the night sky but pricked by thousands of lighted windows.

"The spire of the Empire State Building looks like a needle," I said, "about to inject something into the sky."

"How poetic," Nina said.

"Nina!" Ardis scolded. "Cut it out."

"Sorry. I need a tongue extraction sometimes."

The view to the north was quieter. The buildings were lower, so I saw more sky and even a star. The west windows overlooked Central Park. The sky was faintly pink at the horizon from the sunset. Above the pink was a clear and pure royal blue. The park itself was dark, except for streetlights and car headlights, which streamed like platelets through the park's veins and arteries.

"It's incredible," I said.

"Watch," BeeBee called. She turned on a single row of lights.

Now the skyline was inside with us. BeeBee's father's sculptures were like buildings, throwing long shadows across the floor.

"I hate this part," Ardis said. "I always think they'll come to life."

"And hack our bodies to shreds," Nina said in a sharp, rough voice. "And toss the pieces to the carrion birds hovering outside the windows—waiting, always waiting for their meal."

I grinned and leaned back against a sleeping bag. I had missed this so much—being with other kids, joking around, teasing. I hadn't realized how much I missed it till now.

Chapter Eight

"Stop!" Ardis said with her hands over her ears. "BeeBee, turn on the lights."

"I can't," BeeBee said in a strangled voice. "Aagh. A statue got me."

"It's not funny." Ardis stood up. "Turn the lights on."

"Aaaa!" BeeBee shrieked. "My arms are gone. I'll try to . . . turn . . . them . . . on . . . with . . . my . . . teeth. Aaaa!"

"Turn on the lights! Come on, BeeBee!" Ardis ran toward her and knocked into a statue on the way. The statue swayed. BeeBee yelled, "Watch out! Catch it!" But Ardis kept running.

The statue rocked like a bowling pin. BeeBee started to go to it, and so did I—it was halfway between us—but the statue's swings got shorter, and it wobbled itself back into position. Ardis snapped on the light, and the shadows disappeared.

Nina was laughing so hard, she could hardly talk. "Hack you to bits," she gasped.

"If a statue went down," BeeBee said, "it would fall apart. They're delicate."

Ardis didn't look at us or say anything. She collapsed on the floor and stared at her shoelaces.

It reminded me of times with Freda and Tracy when two of us ganged up on one. I hated when I was the one. I used to do what Ardis was doing now—keep quiet. It only got worse if you showed how hurt you were.

When I was one of the attackers, I used to feel extra safe, but afterward I'd feel terrible.

Before tonight, I couldn't have imagined anybody teasing Ardis. She had seemed untouchable. But not now, and I felt closer to her—she didn't seem so different from me. But I didn't know what to do to make her feel better.

"I'm bored," Nina said.

Ardis put her paper plate and fork into the shopping bag from the restaurant. "Did Liam ask you to Grad Night yet?" Her voice was friendly, like nothing had happened. She was good at this. She didn't need me to fix things up.

Nina shook her head. "He says I should ask him. But then I think he'll say no, just for a joke."

He had asked *me*, in one of the notes I'd gotten. And Carlos, BeeBee's boyfriend, had asked me too. Ardis's boyfriend, Russ, hadn't—unless he'd written one of the anonymous notes.

What would Nina and BeeBee do if they knew? Would they have to like me anyway?

"Who are you going with, Wilma?" BeeBee asked.

"I don't know yet."

"That means nobody asked," Nina said.

Boy, was she wrong. I could have said so, but I wanted the subject to dry up and go away.

"They will," Ardis said loyally.

"I heard they already did," BeeBee said. "Suzanne Russo told me twenty-five boys asked her on Tuesday."

"Really?" Ardis asked. "Twenty-five?"

"Uh-huh." Forty actually. "A lot of them were anonymous," I added.

"You should go with him—Anonymous," Nina said. "He probably dances better—"

"Twenty-five!" Ardis said. "Congratulations!"

BeeBee said, "If twenty-five boys asked me, I'd put it on a T-shirt. I wouldn't let—"

"Who were they?" Nina asked.

"She probably can't remember all of them," Ardis said.

"Try," Nina said.

She was worried about Liam. I named some boys who didn't have girlfriends.

"Who else?" Nina said.

"Ovideo, Benjy . . ."

"Can you imagine kissing Benjy?" BeeBee said. "Your whole face would be wet."

I thought he was kind of cute, actually, like a bulldog is cute in a slobbery way.

"Who else?" Nina repeated.

"Um, Will . . ."

"Will and Wilma," BeeBee said. "That works. He's cute—"

"Shut up, BeeBee," Nina said. "Who else?"

"I'm running out of memory. Daniel . . . Ricky Greiner . . ."

Nina prompted. "Liam? Carlos? Russ?"

"No," I lied. "None of them."

"They could be Anonymous," Nina said.

"Carlos wouldn't do that," BeeBee said. "He's too faithful."

No, he wasn't.

BeeBee said, "You want to hang out with Benjy the Slobberer? Or maybe with Furry Eyebrow?"

That was Jared. They'd think I was nuts for doing

anything with him, but telling them would at least change the subject. "Actually, I'm going to the zoo with Jared on Sunday."

"Oh," BeeBee said.

"Do you like him?" Ardis asked.

No, but I didn't dislike him either. "I don't know. He doesn't drool or anything."

"Not drooling is the perfect recipe for romance," Nina said. "Points off for lousy taste."

Who was she to grade everybody? BeeBee was fun, and Ardis was so poised and nice. But I wasn't sure about Nina. I wanted to like her, maybe just because she looked likable. She was almost as tall as Ardis, with a little puppy fat. Her cheeks were round, her forehead was broad, and her smile was wide. She looked friendly—till she said something.

"Do you like people?" I asked her.

"She's nastiest to her friends," BeeBee said.

"When Reggie wants you to like him," I said, "he wags his tail and licks you."

"I prefer Nina's way," Ardis muttered.

"Hey, girls!" Mrs. Molzen's voice erupted from the vestibule below. "Here comes the fuzz." Her head rose out of the stairwell. "Lights out in fifteen minutes."

"Mom . . ."

"I know there's no school tomorrow, and I know a sleepover is no fun if you can't stay up late. But it *is* late. So I want those lights out." She left.

Ardis, Nina, and BeeBee had almost identical nightgowns—T-shirts that went nearly to their ankles. I had pajamas. The bottoms had an elastic waistband. The top had red-plastic heart-shaped buttons. The print was red hearts pierced by black arrows on a yellow background. If the spell hadn't been protecting me, the three of them would probably have thrown me out a window.

Ardis and BeeBee stared, but Nina—of course—spoke. "I know," she said, getting into her sleeping bag. "They're your lucky pajamas."

"What did I say, Bernice Beryl?" BeeBee's mother called from downstairs. "Turn those lights out."

"Okay, Mom." BeeBee crossed the loft. She turned out the lights, and the skyline twinkled at us again. We heard the door close downstairs.

It was quiet for only a second. Then BeeBee said, "Guess what."

Nina reached over and touched my arm outside my sleeping bag. "Shh," she said.

"Cut it out, guys," BeeBee said. "They always do this to me, Wilma. I say, 'Guess what,' and they won't say 'What?' They just wait for me to tell them anyway, which I always do, but it takes the fun out of it."

Now they were ganging up on BeeBee. I wondered if they ever ganged up on Nina.

"We're breaking you of a bad habit," Nina said.

"What?" I said to BeeBee. I didn't want to be part of it.

"Thanks," BeeBee said. "You're a pal."

"Spoilsport," Nina said.

"Courageous," Ardis said.

Did she mean the compliment? Aside from the spell?

Ardis went on, "We should all stand up to you once in a while, Nina."

"Oh yeah?" But she didn't sound mad.

"Anyway, what?" I asked.

"Stephanie called me. She's back for a few days, visiting her grandmother. Her school . . ."

I stopped listening. The Stephanie they were talking about, Stephanie Hartman, had moved away last December. She had been friends with BeeBee and Nina and Ardis, but I hardly knew her.

"Can you come, Wilma?" BeeBee said.

"Where? Sorry."

"Counting Grad Night dates?" Nina said. "Listen up. We're going blading with Stephanie tomorrow. Can you come?"

"I don't have skates." And I didn't know how to skate. I didn't want to make a fool of myself. But I wanted to go too.

"No problem," BeeBee said. "You can rent."

I didn't say anything.

"Oh, Lord," Nina said. "We'll teach you how to skate."

"Okay, I'll come." It would be fun, with the three of them for teachers.

They started talking about Stephanie again. I stared up at the faraway ceiling. A wave of homesickness washed over me, taking me by surprise. Wasn't I having a wonderful time?

I missed Reggie. He made me too hot and he shook the bed with his panting, but I missed him. I made a fist around the heart locket I always wore. Inside on the left was a tiny picture of Mom, and on the right was one of Reggie.

I wondered what would have happened tonight if I had been here without the spell. Would they have liked me? I hadn't done anything special, except bring a dog to a sleepover and let him pee on a statue.

If Suzanne had given the old lady her seat (which was hard to imagine), and she had been made popular, she would have been here instead of me. And they would be inviting her skating and liking her exactly as much as they liked me—and she was one of the least likable people on earth.

That made me feel funny. The person in this sleeping bag happened to be me, but it could have been anybody.

But if it had been Suzanne, they would have spent the whole night saying nasty things about kids at Claverford, including nasty things about "beloved Wilma." That would have been the kind of night Suzanne would have wanted.

I was glad I wasn't Suzanne. I'd never act like her. I'd be myself, as I had been tonight, and they'd have to love it. I could stop trying to figure out what made other kids popular. I was popular even if I never acted the part. And I'd be popular forever. After all, why would the old lady give me my wish just to take it away?

"Wilma," BeeBee whispered, "are you awake?"

"She is now," Nina said.

"I'm awake."

"I'm glad you came. It's been the best sleepover I ever had."

"It's been perfect," Ardis said.

Nina added, "Fifty points for great company."

In the dark, I smiled.

Chapter Nine

We didn't spend much time together in the morning because BeeBee had to rush to a class at the Art Students League. Then, in the afternoon, I got to the Chelsea Piers rink early. I stood at the edge and watched, wondering if I'd spend the evening at the hospital having my broken neck put in a cast. A few kids from school were there. It was only half a block from Claverford, so we all knew the place.

Timothy skated by, pretending to fall. He looked like he was about to land and break his back, but he never did. Evadney was skating too, and so was Daphne. Daphne skated well, though weirdly. She didn't seem to have bones—she just oozed around the rink.

They all came over to say hi. I was sitting on a bench, surrounded, when BeeBee and Nina arrived wearing their skates. I looked up from lacing my rented Rollerblades.

"Make them tight." Nina pointed at my boots. "It

gives you an illusion of security."

"Steph!" BeeBee yelled.

"Beeb!" Stephanie glided to us from across the street. She hugged BeeBee. "Neen!" She hugged Nina. I smiled at her, but she ignored me.

"Remember Wilma?" BeeBee said. "I told you about her on the phone. Isn't she great?"

I smiled again. "Hi."

She looked at me blankly. "Hi. Where's Ardis?" Stephanie spoke very fast: Hi-where's-Ardis. It sounded like one word.

"She had to go to the dentist," Nina said. "She forgot, and her mother wouldn't let her out of it."

"I'll-yell-at-her-for-having-cavities-why-aren't-you-blading?" Stephanie said in one breath.

"Wilma's been living on Pluto," Nina said. "It's a pain, but we have to show her how to skate."

"She makes up for it," BeeBee said. "You'll see."

Stephanie gave me the blank look again, the way you'd look at a mushroom. Wasn't the spell working?

"Up, monster," Nina said, holding her hands out to me.

I took Nina's hands and got up. The wheels rolled out from under me, and I sat down again—on the ground, with Nina on top of me.

"Sorry," I said.

"That's all right. I love having a zipper in my eye."

"I kind of wanted to skate like we used to," Stephanie said. "I missed you guys."

"Go ahead. I'll watch." I could sit on the bench and pretend to be exhausted from so much fabulous blading.

"You don't mind?" BeeBee said.

"Nope."

"Ten points for unselfishness," Nina said. "See, Steph, that's what she's like."

Stephanie gave me a half smile and skated away. Nina and BeeBee followed her.

Was I imagining that Stephanie didn't like me?

They talked while they skated. When they passed my bench, Stephanie turned her head to look at me. They were talking about me.

They went around for a while and then came for me.

"The moment has come," Nina said. "You're blading."

BeeBee sat on my left. "Put your arm over my shoulder."

Nina got on my other side. They supported me to the edge. When I stepped down into the rink, I almost toppled Nina and BeeBee, but Stephanie straightened me from behind.

"You're such a klutz," Nina said. "It's hard to believe you know how to walk."

They skated me around the rink. Mostly I glided along, carried by their power, but I tried to move my feet a little. Stephanie, who was skating rings around us, said in a rush, "I-can't-believe-how-patient-you're-being-Neen."

BeeBee said, "Don't be fooled. She's as nasty as ever."

"Nasty, but patient. It's weird." Stephanie looked at me again.

"Sorry for slowing you down," I said to everybody.

"Hey!" BeeBee said. "What are friends for?"

Stephanie skated away.

"She's mad," BeeBee said.

"Why?"

"She's acting like a dope," Nina said.

"She's jealous because we invited you," BeeBee said. "She wanted to be alone with us."

"But if she'd give you a chance," Nina said, "she wouldn't mind."

"Did she say she doesn't like me?"

"She said she doesn't like you or dislike you," Nina said. "She doesn't get it—why everybody likes you so much."

But she should have liked me. She shouldn't have been able to stop herself. My stomach lurched a little. Was the spell ending? Was this how it would end, one person at a time? Who would be the next to go?

They skated me around two more times, and then Nina deposited me at the rink wall.

"I think we should skate with Stephanie some more," BeeBee said.

"Skate!" Nina told me. "Practice! Or you'll never make the Olympics." They skated away.

They still liked me. So what was going on?

My right leg started to go out from under me. I bent down and clutched the wall. After a few minutes, I let go and straightened up. Then I inched along, feeling like I needed a cane or, better yet, a walker.

"Give me your hands. I'll pull you."

It was Timothy, class funny man, blading backward in front of me. He'd take my hands, flip me over his head, and holler, "Timber." I shook my head.

"I won't hurt you," he said. "I promise."

"I'll do it." Evadney skated up and held out her hands. I took them, and she started pulling me.

"Lift your feet," Timothy said.

"That's good," Evadney said. "But stop looking down. Good. Very good! Now I'm letting go of your hands. You're on your own."

I was skating—really skating! Stephanie, BeeBee, and Nina passed us, holding hands and skating in step with each other—left foot, right foot, never falling out of step.

"Way to go, Wilma," BeeBee called as she whizzed by.

"Faster, girl!" Nina yelled.

Stephanie didn't look at me.

I tried to go faster. I put some push into my glide, like everyone else did. It worked! I grinned, and pushed even harder.

Disaster struck. I tripped and pitched forward. I tried to save myself. I waved my arms like a windmill and sort of ran with the skates—I must have looked like an animated cartoon. Then I went down. I shot along the ground for a few feet, scraping my helmet and the side of my jaw on the concrete. Then I skidded to a stop.

Chapter Ten

BeeBee got to me first. "Are you okay?"

I sat up. My face stung. Everyone from Claverford plus Stephanie stood around me. "Am I bleeding?"

Nina crouched in front of me. "Not much. It's a good thing you had the helmet."

My T-shirt was filthy. I had made an idiot of myself. I started to undo my skates.

"Don't do that," Nina said. "You have to skate some more, or you'll never get on a horse again."

So I stood up, and Nina and BeeBee and everyone else from Claverford made me skate around the rink a few more times till I began to feel sort of comfortable again. I skated solo, but they all came with me, hovering. Everybody, that is, except Stephanie.

When Nina let me stop skating, we went to a café in the indoor part of the pier. Stephanie came too.

We took a booth. I sat on the outside, next to BeeBee.

Nina faced me, with Stephanie on the inside.

Nina said, "So—is California worth leaving us for?"

"You know I didn't want to go. At first, I was so home-sick, I was constantly in tears. Every night, I'd cry . . ."

How did she talk so fast and still manage to say each word? Why did she avoid looking at me? And then when she did look, why did she stare?

". . . but now Mom's letting me take this course in psychic healing. I go twice a week after school, and when my friend Keisha sprained . . ."

Then I got it. Her blank stares were exactly the way everybody had looked at me after Ms. Hannah read the dog essay. Stephanie still saw the same Wilma everybody used to see.

But why?

They were all engrossed in Stephanie's tales of the West Coast. I felt left out for the first time since I'd gotten my wish.

So at a pause I jumped in. "How come you talk so fast?" I knew I was attacking her, but I was mad that the spell wasn't working and she didn't like me.

"Yeah," Nina said. "You haven't slowed down from the speed of light yet."

"I thought they were so laid back in California," BeeBee said.

"They must think you're an East Coast freak," Nina said. "The mile-a-minute mouth."

Stephanie stared at us. Then she said, "Let me out." Nina stood, and she slid out. "I'm sorry I ever—" She was fighting to keep from crying. "—I couldn't wait to see— I missed you so mu—" She turned and ran.

I had gotten them to gang up on her. I felt like a total louse.

Nina stood up. "I'll go get her."

"No, I'll go," I said. "It's my fault." I wanted to tell her I was sorry.

"Yeah," BeeBee said. "You go. You'll make her feel better."

I ran out of the café. "Stephanie!"

She turned, and turned away again when she saw it was me.

I caught up to her. "I'm sorry. I shouldn't have said that."

"You're right, but it doesn't matter."

"It does matter. It was mean. But I'm really not trying to take BeeBee and Nina away from you."

"They-already-are-away-I-don't-live-here-anymore."

"I know, but we can all be friends."

"No-*we*-can't." She slowed down her blast of words. "Because . . . I . . . don't . . . live . . . here . . . anymore.

Am . . . I . . . speaking . . . slowly . . . enough . . . for . . . you?"

I nodded.

"Maybe you're as incredible as they say, even if you jumped on me for no reason. But why do you care about me? I'm leaving in a couple of days."

I shrugged. "I don't, I guess." This was true. I didn't want to be friends with Stephanie the way I wanted to be with Ardis, for example. "It's just that at Claverford they all—"

"I'm not at Claverford."

Oh.

Aaah. That was it. The old lady made me popular at Claverford. That was why Stephanie didn't like me. What a relief. The spell was still working. I was still popular—at Claverford. And Claverford was all I cared about. "I'm sorry I was mean. Can't you come back? Nina and BeeBee want you to."

"Well, I don't want to." She muttered something under her breath that sounded like a fast chant. I caught "forgive" and "love" and "level." Then she said, "Tell Neen and Beeb I'll call them. Tell them I'm not mad."

I headed back to the café. I should have realized. I knew I wasn't the most popular kid in the world. Only at Claverford, just like I asked for.

Only at Claverford! I tripped and almost fell again. If that was it, if that was really why Stephanie didn't like me, then—then—the spell was almost over, because I wasn't going to be at Claverford much longer. In two weeks we went to Grad Night, and the Monday after that we graduated. And next year I'd be at Elliot. I had sixteen more days of popularity. Then the wish would evaporate, and everything would go back to the way it used to be. Forever.

Chapter Eleven

I gave Nina and BeeBee Stephanie's message and said I had to go home. At the subway station I took the first train that came, even though it wasn't my train. I walked from car to car, looking for the old lady. I had to find her and fix my awful mistake.

I had been so stupid. She had offered to make me one of the in crowd, which exists at any school. Instead, I got my dream come true—for three weeks!

As soon as we graduated, the kids who liked me now wouldn't anymore. BeeBee and Nina would care that I had been mean to Stephanie, their real friend, and Ardis would remember how I had terrified her with Reggie. I'd go back to being ignored. And the dog jokes would start up again.

The old lady wasn't on the train, and she didn't get on at any of the stops. She didn't seem to, anyway.

But she might not always look like an old lady. She might be able to take whatever form she chose. She could be the toddler in the stroller across from me. Or she could be the conductor who was coming into our car right now.

I got off at the last stop and waited for a train going the other way. On the ride back, I calmed down a little. Maybe I'd misinterpreted everything. Maybe there was another reason Stephanie didn't like me. Maybe she was immune to spells. Maybe I wasn't under a spell at all. Maybe the old lady was only a coincidence, and I had just naturally become popular that day. I had waited long enough.

Yeah, right. Outside Claverford that morning I was unpopular. One step inside and I was popular. Very natural.

It was a spell. And it was going to end.

Being left back would solve the problem. If my theory was right, the sixth and seventh graders would go on loving me. I could be popular all my life; I'd just have to stay in middle school. I'd be twenty-five and still going on sleepovers. I'd be married and still in eighth grade. I'd be in the same class with my own children. And then my grandchildren.

Sunday. Fifteen more days of popularity.

When I got to the Central Park Zoo, Jared was waiting for me at the ticket kiosk. I had never seen him in anything but the Claverford uniform for boys— blue blazer, gray slacks, white shirt, and maroon-and-blue-striped tie. Today he was wearing jeans and a T-shirt. Except for his one eyebrow, he looked okay. I was wearing jeans too, and my red zipper-neck T-shirt that I love, except Mom made me put a cardigan over it because it was cool out, and the only one I had that wasn't too heavy was an ugly bright green.

"Hi," Jared said, smiling at me. "You look good."

I smiled back, thinking he should never smile. The eyebrow above and the smile below made an almost complete circle.

"I look like a lollipop," I said.

His smile widened. "They're feeding the sea lions in two minutes," he said.

I love the sea lions. They have so much fun, you don't feel sad that they're in captivity. But I didn't like the announcer for their performance. After he made the sea lions hold their fish in their teeth till he gave the command to eat them, he told us this was proof they were smarter than dogs. He said you could never get a dog to hold its food like that.

"I could," I said. "I could train Reggie to hold on to a treat for as long as I told him to."

"Can he do tricks?"

The show ended while I told Jared about Reggie. We sat on a bench facing the sea lions' pool. I explained all the things Reggie could do, and Jared listened, really seeming interested. Unless the spell made his eyes stay on mine, made him laugh in the right places, made him keep saying, "Go on. What else?"

When I finished telling Reggie stories, he said, "Reggie loves you. He must think you're great."

"I love him too, and he's great."

"Right. It's like the seals. Their trainers are kind, so they think humans are terrific. But a baby elephant whose mother was killed by a hunter would think we were terrible."

I had never thought about it that way.

He added, "Maybe they'd both be right." He stood and put out his hand to pull me up. I took it, thinking he would let go when I was standing, but he didn't.

There was nothing wrong with his hand. It wasn't

clammy or anything, but I imagined what Suzanne would say if she saw us—"Sweater Girl and Eyebrow Boy Hold Hands." That's what she'd say. I felt more on display than the animals.

Chapter Twelve

"I hate this sweater," I said. "I'm taking it off." Jared would have to let go of my hand. I could put up with being a little chilly.

"What's wrong with the sweater?" he asked.

"It's too green."

"Give it to me."

I handed it over, and he tied it around his shoulders. It looked like he was wearing a cape. It looked dumb.

"It looks as bad on you as it did on me." I wished he'd take it off. It was embarrassing. "Give it back."

"No. It matches my toenail polish."

Automatically I looked at his feet. Which were in sneakers.

"Gotcha." He was grinning again.

I grinned too. I couldn't help it. He was funny, even if he was crazy.

"Let's watch the penguins eat," he said, "unless you want to study *Hamlet*."

"Penguins. I had time to study last night."

The penguins were behind glass. When they ate, they lifted their heads and opened their mouths wide like baby birds.

I said, "I guess if they don't catch their own food, they never have a chance to grow up."

"Ancient hunters might feel the same way about us," Jared said. "We don't hunt for our food, so to them we'd be like children."

He said the most amazing things.

"What do you want to be someday?" I asked as we left the building. I wondered because of the ideas he came up with.

He blushed. "A writer. What do you want to be?"

Why was he blushing? It wasn't like he wanted to be a terrorist.

"A vet," I said.

"Are you going to Elliot next year?"

"Yeah. Are you?"

"Yup. We'll be together again."

Well, that's okay, I thought, surprising myself. He was nicer than I expected.

Now we were by the polar bears. My favorite place.

Everybody's favorite place.

Their pool is built into a hill with a glass wall on one side. At ground level, you see the bears plunging through the water, and when you walk up a flight of stairs, you see them coming up for air or lumbering around on the rocks.

"They're so adorable," I said.

"They have big heads," Jared said. "I once read that the animals we think are the cutest have the biggest heads. They remind us of human babies."

How did he know this stuff? "Like pandas?"

"They're the ultimate," Jared said. He took my hand again.

This time, I let him keep it. It wasn't a lifetime commitment.

"It's funny," he said. "I don't usually like popular girls. But I guess it makes sense in your case, because I liked you before you became so popular."

"You did?"

"You know I did. Right after Christmas, your friend Suzanne Russo—"

"She's not my friend."

"I see you together some—"

"We live in the same building."

"Oh. Anyway, she wanted to copy from me on a

French test. I said yes, if she'd tell you I liked you."

"She never said anything."

"She's a creep. In college she's going to major in Creepology."

I laughed. "She'll get straight As."

We watched two bears play with a red rubber ball. Had Jared really liked me before the wish? He might lie, the way Suzanne had, thinking I'd like him better for it.

I looked at him, wearing my stupid sweater. Here was someone who wouldn't lie. Here was someone who liked *me*, the real me, the before-the-spell me. And when the spell ended, maybe he'd go right on liking me.

He continued, "So after nothing happened from Suzanne, I was scared to do anything else. But then, last week, when everybody was writing you notes and trying to sit next to you, I thought, if they can do it, so can I. So I wrote the note about the zoo." He paused. "And a couple more notes."

"That you didn't sign. Which ones?"

"I'm not telling. This was the important one. So far."

Did he write one of the anonymous invitations to Grad Night? I hoped not. Even more, I hoped he wouldn't ask me in person. I didn't want to go with him. He was growing on me, and maybe we could be friends.

But this was my only chance to go with somebody cute, somebody popular. And I didn't want to make him feel bad by saying "no" to his face.

The bears had stopped playing and were snoozing on the rocks.

"Jared?" He was the one to ask about popularity. He could probably quote some article that would explain everything. "Why do you think some girls are popular and some aren't?"

He was quiet for a minute. "I don't know, but the popular girls are usually locked together in bunches and you can't separate them. Want to go to the bird and monkey house?"

"Sure."

As we walked over, he added, "I once read that the most *most* popular kid—somebody like Ardis—hardly ever grows up to be anything special. Like she wouldn't invent time travel or paint an important picture." He blushed again. "I don't mean you. You just became popular. You haven't been that way all along."

Yeah. It wouldn't apply to someone who was only popular for a month, either.

Jared pushed open the door to the Tropics building. Birds don't interest me much, but the monkey room was fun. We watched two monkeys groom a third.

"That one"—Jared pointed at the one who was being groomed—"looks like he's at the dentist."

He was right. The monkey looked patient, unhappy, numb. "Yeah, and that one"—I pointed at the one doing the heavy grooming—"is the dentist, and the other one is his helper. They should be wearing white gowns and rubber gloves."

We watched the whole operation. I had never had such a good time at the zoo before. I fought back a giggle. If I told Jared, he'd say he once read that boys with one eyebrow were the best companions at zoos.

When we were sure the patient was resting comfortably, we left the zoo and walked into the park. The path through Central Park leaving the zoo is lined with benches, and the benches were filled with portrait artists and caricaturists. We watched them work for a while. I wandered around, but Jared stayed near a caricaturist—Antoinette, according to the flamboyant signature on her samples.

"I've always wanted to see what one of them would do to me," he said.

Antoinette was drawing a man with a long face. Only in the caricature his face was so long and narrow that his eyes and mouth could barely fit inside it.

Jared laughed. "That's so funny. Maybe I should do it."

How could he? "Why pay somebody to make you look bad?"

"Not bad—funny. Would you mind waiting?"

I didn't want him to do it, but I also wanted to see what Antoinette would come up with. I'd never seen a caricaturist draw someone I knew.

"All right. Go for it."

Antoinette handed the drawing to her customer, saying, "You're done. I outdid myself."

"Can you do me now?" Jared asked.

"Pay me first, and remember, you asked for it." She waited for Jared to hand over his money.

He paid her and sat on the bench, grinning.

She stared at him for a minute, then extended her arm with her charcoal pencil held vertically. She looked at Jared down the length of her arm and turned the pencil horizontally. Then she drew an egg shape, with the wide end on top.

After that, she marked off where his eyes, nose, and mouth would go. The caricature part began when she put in his forehead. She made it look like an overhanging story on a house—it jutted way out in front of the rest of his face. His eyes were lost underneath, just dark holes. Then she worked on his mouth, which she made narrower than it actually was. After his mouth, she added detail to his nose. She got the shape right, but she drew it too small too. Next, his eyebrow.

Jared has thick, curly brown hair, and his eyebrow hair is curly too. She made it bristly, like barbed wire, as if he had coarse, kinky bristles crawling up his forehead.

I was furious with her. If it weren't for his eyebrow, Jared would be cute. His eyes aren't huge, but they're totally alert. His nose is straight, not too small, not too big. His lips are thin, and I like that. All he needed was tweezers.

She drew in his ears. They were okay. But then she made the hair on his head like his eyebrow, only longer. Now he looked like he was being electrocuted.

The crowning touch came when she started shading. She left his forehead pure white and put the rest of his face in shadow. This made his forehead, bordered by writhing antennae, seem to stick so far out that it cast a shadow over the rest of him, possibly down to his shoes, which were off the page.

"You're done." Antoinette sprayed the drawing with a can labeled "Fixative." "I outdid myself."

Jared came around to see. "It's terrific! Look, Wilma. My eyebrows are a riot."

Antoinette took the caricature away from him and slid it into a big envelope. "How about your girlfriend?"

she said. "You want to give her a gift she'll never forget?"

A caricature of me? No way.

His girlfriend? Jared One Eyebrow's girlfriend? Double no way.

Chapter Thirteen

"You want to?" Jared asked. "I have enough money."

I shook my head.

"Oh. Okay." But I could tell he was disappointed.

Antoinette scanned the area for customers. "Tell you what. I'll do her for half price."

"You will?" Jared looked delighted. "You're sure you don't want to, Wilma? If you do, we'll both have souvenirs."

I did not want a caricature of me as a souvenir.

But I didn't want Jared to know how much all this embarrassed me. Especially, I didn't want him to know that he embarrassed me. He was still wearing my sweater as a cape and holding his revolting caricature tenderly.

He was nuts, but he looked so hopeful, as hopeful as Reggie before mealtime. I couldn't spoil his day. Anyway, how bad could it be? It took just a few minutes, and nobody from school was around to see.

"Okay," I said. "But if you ever tell anybody about this, I'll . . ."

"I won't. I'll go to my grave—"

"Pay me first. And remember, you asked for it."

I sat on the bench where Jared had been, and instantly it was worse than I expected. I faced out, so everybody who passed by could see me. I hadn't thought about that when Jared was sitting here. I felt like a spotlight in the sky was focused on me. My face heated up. If I fainted, Antoinette would just draw me sideways, with my tongue hanging out.

She held out the pencil again.

"Why do you do that?" I asked, to delay things. Maybe she'd talk and forget about drawing.

"Explanations aren't included in the price."

Jared laughed.

"I do it to compare the length and width of your face."

She started drawing. I started panicking. What was she doing? Was she already turning me into a joke?

"Are you all right, Wilma?" Jared said.

I pasted on a smile. "I'm fine. How does it look?"

Antoinette didn't seem to mind if her victim talked. She went on drawing.

"She hasn't done much yet." Then he added, "Wait.

That's good." He grinned. "She just put in your shoulders."

What was wrong with my shoulders? I forced myself not to dash to the easel and tear off the page with poor mutilated me on it.

A few centuries passed. I sat. People walked by, looked, did not gasp, and walked on. A woman and her son, about nine, stopped and watched. The boy stuck his teeth out at me.

Oh no. My big beaver teeth. I clamped my lips together, but I was sure it was too late.

Antoinette stood back from the caricature and studied it. "You're done. I outdid myself."

I jumped up and zoomed to the other side of the easel.

The first thing I saw was my teeth, popping out of my mouth, big and squared off as piano keys. My whole face receded behind those teeth, except for my lips, which smiled insanely around my bicuspids and incisors and molars and fangs and tusks.

Then I saw my shoulders. In themselves they were fine. But they cradled my head. No neck. None. My head was like a golf ball resting on a tee. Like an egg in the palm of your hand. Like a horror movie.

Jared's voice got through. "—super. It's even better than mine. Don't you love it?"

I nodded. Yes, I don't love it. I hated it.

"Never before in history," Jared said. "There's never . . ."

If Ripley saw this, he'd put me in a museum.

". . . been a popular girl before who would do this, who wouldn't be too scared of how she'd look. The most popular kid at Claverford. No wonder."

He was serious. He actually liked me better than before, and he thought other kids would too. I was totally confused.

※　※　※

We left the park. Jared took my hand again, and we walked along Central Park South. He was going to walk me to my apartment and then get the subway home. We went a block or so without talking. I was thinking about how I didn't act popular. Like I should have turned Jared down when he asked me to the zoo, and I shouldn't be holding hands with him, and I definitely should have said no about the caricature.

"Wilma . . ."

"What?"

"Could we trade caricatures? You can have mine if I can have yours."

I took my drawing out of its envelope. Suppose it

weren't me? If it weren't me, then I'd think the smile was insane but infectious, and the eyes, although they were too small, were friendly. And the face itself was heart shaped, which would have been pretty if you could ignore the teeth and the lack of neck, which of course you couldn't. But on the real me, you might be able to, if you tried.

"Could we?"

I should give it to him, since he liked it. But now I didn't want to part with it. I was getting to enjoy it too.

"Let me see yours again," I said.

He showed me. This time I liked his. It was just a joke. It wasn't mean. Jared's face was good-natured under the attic of his forehead.

"Do you think we could find a copy place open on a Sunday?" I asked. "Then we can have one of each of us."

"Let's look."

We had to walk at least a mile, but we found one. Although I was nervous about showing my caricature to the clerk, I was brave and handed it over first.

"Cool," he said. "You want poster size?"

I nodded, and he took the drawing to the back of the store. A minute later, my face with the clerk's legs sticking out from under it advanced toward us. Being enormous intensified the drawing. It came at you. My teeth gobbled you up. I laughed.

"We should get as many copies as we can afford," Jared said. He giggled. "For posterity."

We emptied our wallets. Between us, we had enough for subway fare plus two poster-size copies, two regular-size ones, and one half-size reduction for each of us.

Jared gave me his original drawing plus one poster and his half-size copy. I did the same, and the clerk rolled them into cardboard tubes. Then we headed for the subway. I'd get on the uptown train, and he'd ride downtown to Brooklyn. We walked, holding hands and clutching our tubes.

I shouldn't have made him promise not to tell anybody about the caricature. It was too good to keep secret.

"I don't care if you tell people about the caricature of me," I said. "I changed my mind."

"You can hang mine from a blimp. You can hang it on a banner outside Claverford." He paused. "You could hang the small one in your locker at school. I could do the same thing with yours. Um, can I?"

That would mean he was my boyfriend. People would see the drawings, and that's what it would mean. In three weeks the spell was going to end and I'd have Jared Fein for a boyfriend, which wouldn't help me at all.

And I'd never even had a crush on him. I had a crush on Carlos, and before him, I had a crush on Terence. I liked Jared, but did I *like* him?

I thought about the time I was stuck in the elevator with Carlos. He'd been rude, refusing to talk to me. But then, the instant I became popular, he wrote me a note asking me to Grad Night, even though he had a girlfriend.

It would be fun to be stuck in an elevator with Jared. He'd tell me how people stuck in elevators behaved, or how fast they were rescued, or something else I'd never thought of.

The subway was a block away.

"Hey, Wilma," Jared said. "I asked you something. Did you hear me?"

I nodded and then I said, "Do you want to go to Grad Night with me?"

Chapter Fourteen

He grinned hugely. "Is that instead of putting my picture in your locker or in addition to?"

I grinned back. "In addition." In for a penny, in for a pound, as Mom would say. "I'll tape it up under Reggie's."

We went down the subway stairs and through the turnstile. Then we stood there. A homeless woman was sleeping on a piece of cardboard a few yards away. On the uptown local platform someone was playing a steel drum and singing.

He was my boyfriend. I had a boyfriend.

"I have to go," he said. "I was supposed to be home fifteen minutes ago." But he didn't move. "I had a girl-friend in the fifth grade. We used to play knock hockey for hours at her house. She'd get mad if I won, and I'd get mad if she won." He laughed. "Do you play knock hockey?"

I shook my head.

"Then we'll have to think of something else." He put the caricature tube on the floor between his legs. "Come here." He held out his hands.

He was going to kiss me in the middle of the Thirty-fourth Street station. All my big moments were happening underground. I put my tube down too, took a step toward him, and gave him my hands.

We were the same height. He extended his head, like a turtle poking out of its shell. His head came toward me, chin first. Our teeth clanked from my beaver teeth sticking out. Our lips met for a second. Wetly. He pulled back. His face was bright red.

"I'll practice," he said. "My brother can . . . Then we'll practice. I have to go." He picked up his tube, smiled at me, and ran away.

As soon as I got on my train, I wondered what I was doing. I should have been figuring out how to stay popular, but instead, I'd chosen one of the least popular kids for my boyfriend.

And what was so stupid about that? I liked him. The spell would end and I'd have a boyfriend I liked who didn't care that it ended.

But everybody else would care, and I cared about everybody else. Maybe I shouldn't have, but I did. I remembered the line in *Hamlet* that Jared had quoted, "To thine own self be true." But who was mine own self? That's what I wanted to know.

☼ ☼ ☼

I got home at four. As soon as I walked in, Ardis called, wanting to hear about my afternoon with Jared. When I told her about the caricature, she wanted a preview before I took it to school tomorrow. I asked her if she could come over.

"We could walk Reggie together," I said, "and you could get to know him better." And she could get to know me better.

I heard her take a deep breath. "Wilma, I am a little bit afraid of dogs. Reggie seems great, but—"

"Reggie wouldn't hurt you."

"It might. Animals hate me."

"Reggie doesn't hate anybody, but never mind. You'll see the caricatures tomorrow."

"Look, I'll come. But if I'm too scared, I'm going home. And if it eats me, my dad is a lawyer and he'll—"

"He won't eat you."

I hung up. What a day! I hadn't had a friend over in months. And I'd never had a boyfriend.

Reggie started barking and then the doorbell rang.

I made him sit and stay, which stopped his barking.

"Where did it go?" Ardis said as I opened the door. "Oh. I forgot how big it is. I have to go now."

"Come on in. Reggie, stay."

"You're sure it's safe?" She inched into our apartment.

"Uh-huh. Do you want to pet him?"

"No thanks."

"He's wagging his tail at you," I said.

"That's because it can't wait to eat me." She laughed nervously. "Can I pet it later?"

"Sure."

"Maybe a year from now?"

"Whenever." Whether or not we're friends then. I reached for his leash. As soon as he realized he was getting an extra walk, he was all over me, jumping, licking, wagging.

Ardis stood back. "Aren't you scared it will knock you over?"

Outside, I let him pull me to the nearest lamppost, but then I made him behave.

"Animals don't like me," Ardis said.

"Reggie likes you."

"I went to horseback-riding camp the summer after sixth grade. The horses hated me."

"They couldn't have."

"They did. On one ride, my horse kept putting its head down to eat grass, and everybody in our bunk got ahead of me, and the counselors didn't notice. I was alone with the horse, and I kept thinking it was going to throw me off and then trample me. That was one horse. Another one walked so near the trees that branches kept hitting me."

I said, "I don't know about horses, but dogs will listen if you're consistent and if you . . ."

Ardis had the same expression people have when they watch a TV program somebody else picked. Polite, and annoyed. But what did she want me to say? Didn't she want to learn about animals? I tried to figure it out. What would I want to hear if I was talking about being scared of something?

At BeeBee's sleepover, when I was uncomfortable about the chopsticks, I wouldn't have wanted anybody to tell me how much fun it was to eat with them, or how easy they were to handle. That would have made me feel stupid, which was what I was making Ardis feel.

"Maybe I like animals too much," I said finally. "I only lasted two nights in sleep-away camp."

Her tuned-out look vanished. "Why?"

"Because I missed our dog, Curly. We had her before Reggie."

"What happened to Curly?"

"She got old." I still wanted to cry when I thought about Curly. "We got Reggie a week after she died. I couldn't stand not having a dog."

Ardis laughed. "I couldn't stand having one." Then she said, "My grandmother got sick a year ago. She's better now, but I was scared. I'd miss her . . . a lot."

She kept doing that—putting herself in the other person's shoes. She might not understand animals, but she understood how people felt. If we couldn't be friends when the spell ended—if it ended—I was really going to miss her.

We reached the entrance to the park, and Reggie started pulling.

"We always run in," I called over my shoulder.

She caught up, and we ran to Sheep Meadow. And there was Celeste, the dalmatian I had sniffed in my essay. I waved to Burton, Celeste's owner, and let go of Reggie's leash. He bounded to her.

"Does that dog bite?" Ardis asked.

"Celeste is doggie sugar, just like Reggie."

While we stood there, she asked me a million questions about Reggie and dogs in general. Did Curly ever bite anyone? How much did Reggie weigh? Why did we get such a big dog? Was I scared of pit bulls?

Did anybody ever bother me when I was out with Reggie, and did it protect me?

"He's a he," I said. "He's not an 'it.'" I hated when people did that.

"Sorry," she said. "Did he ever protect you?"

"He never needed to. He likes people so much, I don't know if he'd realize somebody was trying to hurt me. He might think we were just playing."

On the way home, Ardis said, "Can I hold his leash?"

I gave it to her. It was safe. He doesn't pull on the way back from a walk.

She took it for a second while Reggie sniffed a lamppost, and then she got scared again. But after she gave it back to me, she said, "Did I do it right? Do you think anybody might have thought I was his owner?"

"They might have."

"You must think I'm a wimp."

"You're not a wimp. I'm scared of lots of things." I took a deep breath. "I'm scared people won't like me."

"That's crazy. Nina would take points off. Everybody thinks you're great." She paused. "I think you are."

"Thanks." I wished the spell could drop away, just for a minute or two, so I could see if I was getting anywhere, if she honestly thought I was even a tiny bit great.

"Ardis . . . what makes somebody popular, do you think?"

She thought for a minute. "I wouldn't tell this to anybody but you, and you have to swear to keep it a secret."

I nodded. "I swear. I won't tell."

She didn't look at me while she spoke. "Well, you know I went to elementary school in Chicago, where we lived before."

I hadn't known. I didn't know her till we started at Claverford.

"I was the least popular kid in my class. Nobody liked me. I was taller than anybody else, and they called me The Mountain."

She knew what it was like. It was hard to believe.

"Then, before I started at Claverford, my dad said I could make it different here. So the first day, when we were all new, I figured it was my chance. I was friendly to everybody."

"Hold on." Reggie had stopped to pee, and Ardis had gotten ahead of me.

We started walking again, and she went on. "I smiled at everyone. I felt like a fake, but I couldn't think of anything else to do. I said 'hi.' I said I was nervous about the first day of school, and isn't this cafeteria food crummy, and who are your teachers? And then, that first day, I'll never forget it, I was trying to figure out the combination on my locker, and I heard BeeBee whisper to Stephanie to look at me, I was beautiful. I couldn't believe it. I was extra friendly to BeeBee after that. I would have given her a million dollars if I had it." She giggled. "If she needed it."

"It's that simple?" I said. I could do it, be extra friendly at Elliot next year, except that most of the kids came from Claverford, so they'd already know me.

Ardis nodded and laughed. "Yeah." She shrugged. "Although that was the hardest day of my life. And now sometimes I'm nice to people I don't like or when I really feel like screaming. But it's better than being The Mountain. And . . ." She shrugged again. "Anyway, my parents raised me to be polite."

Reggie began to drag on the leash. We were almost home, and he didn't want the walk to end. "Come on, boy. Why do you think Nina and BeeBee are popular, then?"

"Why are you worried, Wilma? There isn't a single person at Claverford who doesn't think you're . . . I can't think of a word that's good enough. Extremely . . . uh . . . ultra ultra . . . Super likable."

"What do they like so much about me?"

"I don't know. For me it's nothing specific. It's just that it's more fun to be with you, doing anything, than to be with anyone else. Like at BeeBee's sleepover. Like now."

So it didn't matter what I said or did. If the old lady was going to end the spell, couldn't she have helped me some more? Couldn't she have made them all fall in love with my real good points?

"Forget about me. What do you think makes Nina and BeeBee popular?"

"You're completely nuts. Reggie, you should straighten out your friend here. Okay. BeeBee doesn't care about being popular. She ignores it, and that works. And Nina's popular because kids are afraid not to like her—they're scared she'll turn her point system against them, even though she wouldn't."

We turned into my building. I rang for the elevator.

"Do you think I'll get over being scared of Reggie eventually?"

"Sure. Once you got used to him. He'd train you."

"I'll visit you regularly for the next decade."

I wish.

Chapter Fifteen

Ardis looked around. "I like your apartment."

I was surprised. It wasn't fabulous like BeeBee's. Inside the door, next to where we were standing, was a table where we dumped whatever we had when we came in. Right now it was covered with my backpack, a week's worth of junk mail, and today's *New York Times*. From here you could see into the kitchen and the living room. In the living room, the coffee table was piled high with more newspapers and a few books. A quilt was draped across the couch and trailed onto the floor.

It wasn't dirty, just messy. The rug was vacuumed, for example, and Mom didn't let us leave dirty dishes in the sink.

"In our house," Ardis said, "we have to take our shoes off before we come in, and I feel guilty about my smelly feet touching the floor."

We went into the living room. Maud was in our

bedroom studying. Mom was at the soup kitchen where she volunteers.

"Show me the caricature."

"Close your eyes."

The caricatures were in the coat closet. I pulled out the poster-size one of me. I really wanted Ardis to like it, to see it the way Jared and I did.

I held it up against my chest. "Ready."

Ardis opened her eyes. Silence.

"It's interesting?" I giggled nervously.

"It's funny," Ardis finally said. "But you're much prettier."

I was? Really?

She was quiet again.

"It's funny because it's true. My teeth *are* too big, and my neck *is* too short."

"Not like that. It's not noticeable, except to a caricaturist—"

"Or to somebody like Suzanne Russo." And to me.

"Yeah," Ardis said. "Suzanne probably thinks everybody looks like a caricature. And nobody—especially not Suzanne—will understand why you're letting Jared show a drawing of you that's . . ." She searched for a word. ". . . that's not flattering."

I was letting him because it seemed like a good joke to

share with people. But maybe I should call him tonight and tell him I changed my mind. I could give him a real photo of me to put up in his locker.

Ardis sank into Mom's chair. "Look, Wilma. Remember how we talked about popularity before? Well, none of—"

Reggie started barking. The doorbell rang.

Just when Ardis was saying something important. Who could it be, anyway?

"I'll get it," I yelled to Maud. If I didn't answer the door, she'd tell Mom how I made her interrupt her studying.

Ardis said, sounding surprised, "Reggie barks at everyone, not only me."

I dropped the poster on the couch. "Don't forget what you were saying before. I want to hear it."

I opened the door. Suzanne stood there, holding a shrink-wrapped box that Reggie started sniffing. "I didn't know you had company," she said before she even looked in the living room.

She knew.

"Hi, Ardis," she called.

"Suzanne!" Ardis rushed at her. "What are you doing here? Wilma was showing me her videotapes, but before that we were in the kitchen. Let's go back in there. I like it better there."

She was diverting Suzanne from the poster. She was protecting me. That was so nice that a lump formed in my throat.

Suzanne glanced suspiciously into the living room but followed Ardis. Reggie came after us, still interested in Suzanne's package.

"What's that?" Ardis pointed at the box.

"Gourmet dog treats. I came over to give them to your dog." She handed them to me.

"What's a gourmet dog treat?" Ardis asked.

"How should I know?" Suzanne said. "But I'm dying to find out. Open it, Wilma."

I turned the box over and read out loud, "'These elegant treats come in three delicious flavors: venison, organic filet mignon, and free-range chicken.'" I tore off the plastic wrap and lifted the cover. Inside were nine dog biscuits in three shapes—deer, cow, and chicken. I looked at the plastic wrap again. She had paid seven dollars for an excuse to come over.

I found myself feeling sorry for her. "Thanks. Here, Reggie." I gave him a deer, and he trotted off with it.

"What's happening?" Suzanne asked.

"Nothing," Ardis said. "We're just hanging out."

"That's cool." She looked around the kitchen for a second.

Then she leaned toward us and her eyes gleamed. "Did you hear that Mr. Pike sent Daphne to the principal because of her b.o.? And Mr. Winby sent her home?"

I stopped feeling sorry. The worst part of Suzanne's gossip was that I sort of enjoyed hearing about other people's problems. I didn't enjoy the enjoyment though. And I hated knowing that I'd never forget the tidbit. I could forget what six times seven equals or the name of Hamlet's girlfriend, but I'd remember Daphne's body odor forever.

"No, I didn't hear—"

"Thanks for sharing," Ardis said. "But Wilma and I were talking about some personal things, and you won't mind, will you, if we all get together another time?"

"I can't stay anyway. We're having dinner soon." She left the kitchen, but instead of going to the door, she went into the living room. "I heard your mom say you were getting a new TV. How big is the—"

We raced to get to the couch first.

"What's this?" Suzanne picked up the caricature and unrolled it. First she held it out so she could see it better, and then she brought it near for a closer inspection.

"She's memorizing it," Ardis whispered to me.

"This is so neat," Suzanne finally said. "Where did you get it? Who's Antoinette? You're a genius."

"We got it in Central Park."

"You and Ardis?"

"Me and Jared."

"Jared? You mean . . ." She put her finger across the bridge of her nose. "That Jared?"

I nodded.

"You like him?"

I nodded. No hesitation at all.

She nodded with me. "You make a cute couple. He's cute, except . . . He's cute. I could go for him."

"You like the caricature?" I think Ardis tried to keep the astonishment out of her voice, but I heard it.

"Don't you? I mean, I'm no art critic—"

"I love it," Ardis said firmly. "I think it's a riot."

"It's funny? Right. I knew that." She made herself laugh.

"'Bye, Suzanne," I said.

"'Bye." She stopped at our door. "Ardis and I are the first ones to see it?"

"Except Jared."

"Are you going to show anybody else?"

"You'll see," I said.

"Well, 'bye," she said. "I have to go. Dinner." Now she couldn't wait to leave. If her phone was more than two minutes away, she would have a heart attack before she got there.

I locked the door and came back to the living room. "Tell me what you were going to say before."

"It doesn't matter anymore." Ardis shook her head. "I don't believe that. She liked it. I thought she'd start destroying you the second she saw it."

"You know Suzanne. If she thought she could hurt me, she would."

"But she can't?"

Oops! I thought fast. "With you here? With you saying you liked it?" Would she believe me?

"I guess." She grinned. "I like being your fairy godmother."

🌀　🌀　🌀

Jared called that night. The first thing he said was "My brother's going to give me kissing lessons tomorrow. He already told me the Five Rules of Kissing."

"What are they?"

"You'll see."

"Come on. Tell."

"No. I'll tell you after we try them out. Could we do

it after school on Wednesday? That'll give me time to practice."

Try out kissing? That meant kissing. You couldn't try it out without doing it. My heart started pounding, three days ahead of time. "Okay."

"Good. What did your family think of the caricatures?"

"Maud—she's my older sister—thinks we're crazy. She said I should bury them in Central Park, six feet down and under a boulder."

"What did your parents think?"

"My mom wants to get a wallet-size one of me to carry around with her."

"How about your dad?"

"They're divorced. What about your family?"

"Dad says I have good taste in girls."

"What did your brother say?"

"Which one? My older brother, Brad, said he wished he knew a girl like you. Andy—he's five—started to cry when he saw my picture. But he liked yours. He wanted to know if your teeth are really that big."

"What did you tell him?"

"I said they were bigger, and he can't wait to meet you either."

I laughed. "The saber-toothed tigress."

It was fun having a boyfriend.

Chapter Sixteen

Monday. Two more weeks of popularity.

Suzanne must have been on the phone all night, because the first kid I saw in the morning knew about the caricatures. I was mobbed on the way to school. Everybody was dying to see them, and they had a million questions about what it was like to have a caricaturist draw you.

Boys told me they liked the drawing, and it was funny. Girls told me they liked the drawing, and I was brave. Almost everybody told me I was much prettier than the caricature. And I kept saying that was lucky, because you couldn't get much uglier. Then lots of them said, No, you really are pretty.

Maybe everybody should have a caricature done. Then we'd all see how everybody else actually looks. But maybe kids only thought I was pretty because of the spell.

The girls wanted to know all about Jared. I had to

repeat the events of our afternoon together at least a dozen times. Research in case we broke up, I guess.

Then at lunch, when I thought I'd said everything anybody could possibly want to know, Evadney asked, "But what's Jared really like?"

"What do you mean?"

BeeBee said, "I know what she means. It's like Carlos is a total jock, but every so often I see something else inside him. The little boy, maybe."

Evadney nodded.

BeeBee had seen the jock, not the jerk, in Carlos. She hadn't seen the inner creep who'd asked me to Grad Night. The Grad Night date bigamist.

"I don't know," I said. "The real Jared doesn't seem to be hiding. He's out there."

☼ ☼ ☼

I had computer lab for eighth period, and Ms. Jacobson asked BeeBee to show a computer graphics program to a bunch of us while she helped some other kids. Daphne, Nina, Ardis, Suzanne, and I crowded around BeeBee. I was the last one to get there, but Nina made room for me, and I wound up with the best view of what BeeBee was doing.

She had scanned our class picture into the computer

and was fooling around with it. She took Geoff, the shortest boy in eighth grade, and stretched him out, making him so tall that the photo lopped off the top of his forehead. Then she cut out my head and moved it onto the neck of Mr. Winby, our principal.

"Could you do the caricatures?" Ardis asked.

"Sure. Hand them over, Wilma."

I did, and BeeBee showed us how to use the scanner. Suzanne, who had wormed her way in between me and Ardis, kept complimenting BeeBee on everything she did. Then I realized after the fortieth compliment that Suzanne wasn't only sucking up. She was also pointing out that this was a rare event—BeeBee catching on to something ahead of anyone else.

Poisonous.

I wanted to neutralize Suzanne, but I couldn't think of anything to say.

Luckily, BeeBee didn't seem to care. She brought Jared's drawing up on the screen. "Watch." She added shading to his forehead, so it didn't seem to stick out, and she made his hair more natural. Then she moved the cursor to his eyebrow.

She was going to separate his one eyebrow into two. "Don't!" I said. He wouldn't be Jared anymore. "I like that eyebrow."

"It's sexy, isn't it?" Nina laughed.

"It grows on you," I said, laughing too.

"The longer it is, the better it is," Daphne added.

And we all started laughing so hard, we couldn't catch our breath. As we wound down, I noticed that Daphne was looking very pleased with herself for making us laugh.

That is, till Suzanne said, "Jared may have only one eyebrow, but at least he *smells* better than some people." She looked straight at Daphne.

Daphne went on smiling, but all the fun seeped out of it, and a raspberry blush spread across her pale face.

BeeBee said, "Suzanne! That was so mean. That was obno—"

I interrupted. "Does everybody know that Suzanne and I live in the same building?"

"Yeah," Suzanne agreed. "We've known each other forever."

"Well," I said, "last week I was going into the laundry room, and I heard her mother ask a neighbor what to do about Suzanne's bed-wetting."

"That isn't funny," Suzanne said. "You shouldn't tell lies like that about people."

"Points, Wilma," Nina said. "A thousand points."

I looked at Daphne, who was grinning. I saw her take

a deep breath. "You're all standing near me. Do I stink? Do I?"

"No," Ardis said. "You don't."

Well, I had done something. I had struck a blow at Suzanne. Funny how I could do it for Daphne when I had never been able to do it for myself. But maybe I would be able to in the future.

※　※　※

When I got home, Maud told me I'd have to walk Reggie after school on Wednesday because she was going to her best friend Portia's house to study for a big exam. Maud didn't have just plain exams, they were always "big."

"Okay." I never minded walking Reggie. "No. Wait." Jared and I were supposed to practice kissing. "I can't."

"You'll have to. My grades are more important than your social calendar."

I couldn't win. Mom would agree with Maud, especially if I said I couldn't walk Reggie because it would interfere with kissing Jared. "All right," I said.

The phone rang. It was Daphne calling to thank me for helping her out.

"Somebody had to do something about Suzanne," I said, feeling like a hero.

"Uh, how's Reggie?"

"Fine. He's sleeping." I remembered that Daphne had shown me a picture of her sheepdog. "How's your dog?"

"Samson's good. He's chewing on a rawhide bone."

So then we talked about dogs. I found out Samson was ten years old, and they'd gotten him from the sheep-dog rescue organization when he was two.

I found myself asking her if she wanted to walk our dogs together sometime. She did, and we agreed to meet in the park next Saturday morning.

※　※　※

Tuesday. Thirteen more days.

In the morning I left home early so I wouldn't meet anybody on the way to school. The old lady was my best bet for staying popular, much better than the odds of dis-covering an unmagical way to do it.

The train was almost full, but I found a seat. More people got on at the next stop. The man who stood in front of me seemed healthy. It didn't seem possible that the old lady had taken his form. But maybe she had, and he had stationed himself near me because he wanted to see if I'd recognize him—her.

I caught his eye. "Would you like to sit down?"

He nodded. I stood up, and he slid into my seat.

"How did you know?" he asked.

He was the old lady!

"These shoes are new." He extended his left foot. "I have a blister already."

He wasn't the old lady. I smiled weakly at him and turned to face the pole I was hanging on to.

Anybody might be the old lady, and how would I know? I couldn't ask people if I had met them before when they were in the shape of an old lady. They'd call the police, who'd take me to a psychiatric ward for observation.

I must have seemed upset at school, because everybody kept asking me if something was wrong. A sixth grader stopped me in the hall and told me she was there for me. Three girls asked me if I was getting my period. Even Nina got emotional and offered me both her shoulders to cry on.

And I got another poem from Anonymous, the poet who had written to me on the first day.

No smiles today.
Today her long teeth
Are shrouded.
And her eyes

Are quenched.
Even the shape
Of her ears
Is sad today.

My boat will not
Sail today.
Today my kite
Will not fly.
And I am earth
Bound as a stone.

At least I could keep the two poems and show them to my grandchildren as souvenirs of the nanosecond when Granny was popular.

Chapter Seventeen

Wednesday. Twelve more days. In language arts I told Jared that we couldn't have our kissing session because I had to walk Reggie after school.

"Where do you take him?"

"Central Park."

"Ideal." He grinned wickedly. "I was worried about Rule Number Two."

So we agreed to meet under the clock in the lobby after school, and I spent the rest of the day being excited and terrified about my first real kissing experience. I hardly thought about the end of the spell . . . hardly.

"Who are you looking for?" Jared asked in the train on the way home.

"Nobody." I turned to face him.

"I guess I like Rule Number One best," he said.

"What's that?"

"You'll see."

On the walk home, he told me about his brother's first kiss. "In the second grade Brad had a crush on this girl named Tina Delphina. She—"

"That was really her name?"

"You interrupted."

I giggled.

"Yes. That was her name, and she had pigtails and he loved her. On Valentine's Day he decided to kiss her. They were in the school playground and she was talking to her friends. He ran to her, meaning to kiss her cheek. He didn't know about kissing on the lips. Just as he got near her, she turned— Maybe this is the wrong story to tell right now."

"You can't stop now. Tell."

"All right. She turned. He didn't know she was chewing bubble gum. And while she turned, she blew a bubble." Jared started laughing, and I was laughing already. "So he kissed the bubble, and it burst and he had . . ." He was laughing so hard, he had to stop talking. ". . . and he had her bubble gum all over his mouth."

"You're making it up," I gasped between laughs. We were crossing Amsterdam Avenue. My house was a block away.

He shook his head, tears streaming. "No. It's true.

When he pulled away . . . Brad can't stop laughing when he tells this part. When he pulled away . . ." Jared tried to catch his breath. ". . . a long pink strand stretched between them. They were connected by this long pink strand till he got about five feet away from her, and then it broke."

"Then what happened?" We walked into my building.

"I don't know. But Brad hates gum to this day."

Upstairs, Jared was good with Reggie. He didn't mind when Reggie went wild, jumping on him and licking his face all over.

"My sister hates it when he does that," I said. "You can rinse your mouth before we go."

"It's okay. We'll have a three-way saliva exchange."

Please, please let him keep liking me after graduation.

"Rule Number One Hundred," I said. "Always kiss your girlfriend's dog."

"Right."

❀　❀　❀

Were there always so many people in the park? Bikers, strollers, dog walkers, skaters, joggers, toddlers. A clown walking on stilts. People were sprawled across every patch of grass we passed. Jared started whistling.

"We need to be near something I can tie Reggie to."

I had brought rope to attach to his leash so he could roam around after I tied him up.

"I'm looking." He went back to whistling.

"What's over there?" I pointed at a rocky hill.

We climbed it. As Nina would have said, points for privacy, points for a small tree to tie Reggie to, and points off for everything else. Dirt and rock, no grass. And we faced the ugly brick side of a park building.

"Is this okay?" Jared asked, kicking away a jagged piece of beer bottle.

I was still wearing my Claverford uniform, which was going to get filthy and gritty. "Perfect," I said.

"At least we don't have to get dirty." Jared opened his backpack and pulled out a sheet, which he spread on the ground.

I tied Reggie to the tree. He sniffed along the building wall. Jared sat on the sheet and leaned back on his elbow. He patted the spot next to him.

I sat. My heart was beating too fast.

He tugged at my arm to bring me down to him. I lay next to him on the sheet. My hair swung over part of my face. He pushed it away and tucked it behind my ear. I felt hollow with expectation.

And Reggie landed between us, barking and growling. Jared jumped up.

"Reggie! It's okay, boy." I rubbed his ears, which he loves. "Nobody was hurting me." He licked my face and wagged his tail. "It's safe now."

Jared came toward us and Reggie growled again.

"Bad! That's bad! Bad boy!"

Reggie's tail went down, and he licked my face again.

"Now he knows better," I told Jared. "He won't do it again."

"You're sure?" He took a step.

Reggie growled.

I stood up and walked about four feet from the sheet. Reggie followed me, tail halfway down, wagging madly, completely apologetic.

"He's jealous." Jared sat on the sheet again. "And I am too."

"Down, Reggie. Stay." I went back to the sheet. "He won't move." I stretched out next to Jared, my back to Reggie.

He started growling again. I turned around. He hadn't moved, but he was growling furiously.

Jared giggled. "Romantic music."

"He sounds like a small locomotive."

"Well, we're doing Rule Number Four."

"What's that?"

"Having fun." He kissed my nose. A light kiss.

The pitch of Reggie's growl deepened.

"Is he still lying there?" I asked.

"Uh-huh." He kissed me softly on the lips.

I kissed him back. The next kiss was longer. I forgot about Reggie. I forgot about popularity.

By the time we stopped, Reggie was asleep. We must have kissed for more than an hour. We had smiled at each other and laughed, but some of the kisses felt very serious. I had pushed my fingers through his hair. I had even smoothed out his eyebrow.

Jared stopped first. He looked at his watch. "It's five thirty." He kissed me again.

"Mom's home." I sat up. "I better go."

He sat up too. "Me too, I guess."

We kissed. We stood up and kissed. Reggie woke up and started growling again. We folded the sheet, and every time we brought the edges toward each other, we kissed. When we finished, Jared put the sheet away, and I untied Reggie from the tree. He seemed to be all right as long as we weren't kissing, but I made him heel while we walked out of the park.

"So, what are the Rules?" I asked.

"Well, you know what Four is."

"I forgot."

"Okay. Here goes. I told you, Number One is my favorite. It's take your time."

"We did that."

"Two is you have to have a romantic setting. I don't know if we made it on that."

"Not everybody gets to have a dog growling in the background."

We waited for the light on Central Park West.

"True. Three is the kissers should like each other. I ace that one."

"Me too."

We crossed the street.

"Number Four I told you—it should be fun and not too scary. Five is you can kiss with your mouth open or shut."

"That's not a rule, that's a choice."

"Go argue with my brother. Six is—"

"You said there were five Rules."

He blushed. "I didn't want to tell you about Six till we were through."

"What is it?"

"Anybody can stop anytime. No hard feelings. I would have told it to you if anything seemed wrong."

"You didn't mention Number Seven either."

"There isn't a Seven."

"Yes, there is. Sit, Reggie." I kissed Jared, a short one on the lips. "Sixty-sixth Street is a kissing zone." We were at the corner of Sixty-sixth and Broadway, by the subway entrance where he was going to leave me.

"That's a good rule. Tell Reggie to stay."

I did, and we had one more long one. And I smiled all the way home.

Chapter Eighteen

Thursday. Eleven more days.

After school, Ardis came with me to study history at my house. When we got there, Reggie was too busy leaping at me to leap at Ardis. She backed into the kitchen but stood in the doorway, watching us and smiling, which I thought was a good sign.

"It seems like fun," she said. "I wish . . ."

"If a genie gave you one wish, what would it be?" I asked when Reggie calmed down.

"To live forever, I guess. Maybe not to be scared of animals. I don't know. Maybe for my mother not to be such a cleanliness freak. What would yours be?"

I paused. "Maybe for people to like me. Let's work in the kitchen. Maud's in the bedroom. I have to get my history book." I left before she could say anything.

When I came back, we started studying. And I

found out that one of Suzanne's rumors was true—Ardis was awful at history.

"How do you remember which civilization came first?"

"I don't know how. I just do."

"Great. Big help."

"Let me think. We need a memory thing. You know, a nemo . . ."

"A mnemonic device?"

"Yeah. Like, listen. Mesopotamian came first. That's an 'm.' Then Babylonian. That's a 'b.' Assyrian, Egyptian . . ."

Ardis wrote down the initials.

". . . Minoan, Mycenaean, Greek, and Roman. What do we have?"

"M B A E M M G R." She turned her notebook toward me, and we both stared at it.

"Um," I said. "Most Baboons Are Eaten by Mad Mongooses—mongeese?—in Green Robes."

"Everything is about animals with you," she said, laughing. "How's Many Babies Are Eaten by Mad Mothers in . . . uh . . . Gray Raincoats?"

"We must be hungry. 'E' doesn't only have to stand for 'eat.'" I pulled a box of pretzels out of the cabinet over the sink. "Can you think of any more?"

"Give me a minute. . . . Here's one. My Brother

And Every Musical Man Grow Radishes."

"I like it," I said.

"It doesn't have any extra words. I won't go nuts trying to figure out what 'in' and 'by' stand for."

"Okay, so now you just have to remember the sentence."

"That's easy. My Brother And Every Musical Man Grow Radishes."

After that we worked on how long each civilization lasted, and I made her memorize them till she could say them back to me without stopping to think.

Finally she said, "I can't take any more. I'll work on it this weekend. What are you wearing to Grad Night?" She riffled through the pages of the history book. "I wish I could wear this." She pointed at a toga.

"You'd look fabulous. You could wear gold bracelets on your arms above the elbows." She'd be gorgeous. She was gorgeous in the Claverford uniform. She'd be gorgeous times a million.

"Yeah, and I could wear leather sandals with straps that lace up to my knees."

We were quiet, picturing it. Then I said, "What's your dress really like?"

She grinned. "It's not a toga, but it's okay. It's an African print, and it's two-piece, and the skirt is very short. What's yours like?"

I loved my dress. It was dark-blue taffeta. Not the dull Claverford navy, but royal and midnight blue mixed together. Across the front was a scattering of pale dots, like stars in the Milky Way.

"I'll show you." I went into the bedroom, took the dress out of the closet, and went back to the kitchen . . .

. . . and found Reggie sitting next to Ardis with his head in her lap. She had that look you get on your face when a soap bubble touches your arm and doesn't burst immediately, or when a butterfly lands on you— something magical and precious has just happened and you don't want it to end.

Her hand hovered about two inches above his head. She was dying to pet him, but she was still afraid.

"He loves it if you scratch behind his ears," I said.

And she did it!

"He's wagging his tail!" she said, smiling delightedly.

"He likes what you're doing. He likes you." After graduation, please remember I made this possible.

"I like him. I like you, doggie-Reggie."

Reggie wagged his tail a few more times, then stood and shook himself.

"I feel abandoned."

"You shouldn't. It makes it that much more of an

honor when he does come over."

"I guess."

"I think he'd like a pretzel."

"Is it all right? The salt isn't bad for him?"

"It's all right."

She gave him one without flinching, and he trotted off with it. "Is that your dress? What a stupendous color. Oh! I almost forgot. Nina and BeeBee are coming to my house before Grad Night to get ready together. Russ, Liam, and Carlos are meeting us there. Jared could too. You want to come? BeeBee is incredible with hair and makeup."

I nodded. Going to Ardis's would be a fabulous beginning for the Final Triumph of Wilma the Popular.

Chapter Nineteen

Friday. Ten more days.

Ms. Hannah gave our yearbooks out in homeroom. My prepopularity photo smiled dutifully at me from page sixty-seven. Underneath, it said:

> *Wilma Sturtz*
> *Science Club*
> *You can count on Wilma.*

I wondered what they'd write about me now.

There was a saying under each picture. I hunted for Ardis's. There. Under "SGO, Debating Club, Russian Club," her saying was "Sensitive, smart, stunning—spectacular!" And they were right.

Under Nina's photo, it said, "A thousand points for wit and friendship." BeeBee's was "The next Picasso—and she's nice too!" Jared's was "Behind those eyebrows, the pen of a writer." It sounded like he had a ballpoint in his skull instead of brains.

Daphne's wasn't any better than mine. Hers was "We expect a lot from Daphne." Under Suzanne's it said, "The snoop with the scoop. Beware of libel suits!"

I spent the day autographing yearbooks and having mine autographed. I asked everybody to write why they liked me. I wanted to find out how the spell made me seem to them.

In their books, I tried to write why I liked them. In Ardis's I wrote, "My favorite because you're honest and fun and <u>brave</u>!" In Nina's I wrote, "All that's behind your bark is a wagging tail and a wet tongue." To BeeBee—"For putting up with a skating dummy and for not having a fit about Reggie." To Daphne—"I like all dog lovers, especially the ones with a sense of humor."

I held Jared's book for five minutes before I figured out what to say. Finally, I wrote, "I like your Rules, your caricature, the amazing stuff you say—and your eyebrows."

I had to struggle to think of things to write about everybody else, but I didn't lie to anyone. In Suzanne's book I just signed my name.

My book was passed around so much that I didn't get to look through it till sixth period, when I held it in

my lap while Ms. Singer went over math problems. I
checked first to see what Jared had written. Under his
picture were the words "See back cover." I turned to the
back and found two poems. The first one was:

> *She asks why I like her.*
> *Might as well ask*
> *Why I breathe.*
> *Maybe tomorrow I won't*
> *Breathe or like her*
> *Anymore.*
> *Maybe tomorrow the tides*
> *Will stop.*
> *Maybe tomorrow will bring*
> *No more rainbows.*
> *Maybe tomorrow*
> *She will stop*
> *Asking useless questions.*

It was signed, "From Jared Fein." The next one was:

> *I like you because . . .*
> *We held hands and I liked it*
> *We kissed and I liked it*
> *We even talked and I liked it*

I like you because . . .
We held hands and you liked it
We kissed and you liked it
We talked and you liked it
I like you because . . .
You're kind to dogs
And seals
And me
I like you because . . .

He was the poet! Now that I knew, it made the other poems even better. They were beautiful. I felt like a movie star, having poems like that written to me.

I turned to the front of the book. The pages were so full of writing, you could hardly see the photos. I found Ardis's picture again. In the margin above her face, she had written, "You goof! I like you because you're Reggie's owner! And many, many more reasons. Love, Ardis."

What reasons? I wished she had told me!

Daphne had scribbled over her photo, so I guess she thought it was bad. She wrote, "Thanks for sticking up for me."

When I read the other kids' messages, I was bewildered. What they wrote didn't make sense. They thought they were writing about me, but they weren't. A sixth grader wrote inside the front cover, "I like you because you know what I'm really like." But I hardly knew her! Erica wrote that I never made judgments about her. Which was true, but only because I didn't know her well enough to make them. I think BeeBee summed up what everybody was saying. She wrote, "I like you because you like me through and through."

Then I figured it out. I was like a celebrity. People felt about me the way you feel about an actor you love. You see his movies and then you read about him in magazines. You find out he likes the same kind of music as you, or maybe he has a dog. And then you discover that his parents got divorced when he was nine, and yours did too. You start thinking, If he knew me, he'd really like me. Pretty soon you feel he does know you, and if he saw you on the street, he'd recognize you as his soul mate, and you'd fall into each other's arms.

My celebrity status made them imagine I knew their secret, best selves. But to stay a celebrity, I had to find the old lady. And she wasn't anywhere.

☼   ☼   ☼

Saturday. Nine more days.

In the morning, I met Daphne in Sheep Meadow in

Central Park. Her sheepdog, Samson, kept trying to herd Reggie while they played.

"It's easy to have friends if you're a dog," I said. "If you don't bite and you smell right, you're in."

"Yeah. Nobody says your ears are pointy so I don't like you." Daphne sat on the grass.

I joined her. "Are you studying for finals?"

"Yeah. This is the last daylight I'll see this weekend."

"Mom isn't letting me talk on the phone," I said. "When it rings, she picks it up and sounds like an answering machine. 'I'm sorry. Wilma can't come to the phone right now.'"

"At least your phone rings. I don't know why you envy dogs. You make friends faster than they do. Everybody's your friend."

"Everybody at school."

"Who else is there?"

Nobody else.

We watched the dogs. Reggie had picked up a stick and was prancing off with it, chased by Samson.

"I'm not just studying," she added. "I'm also working on my valedictory speech."

"What are you going to say?"

"I've been trying to think of a way to say how much

I've hated Claverford without anybody knowing that's what I'm saying."

"Why can't they know?"

"Because they look at the speech ahead of time."

"They do? Who?"

"The graduation committee. Ms. Hannah's on it."

"Isn't that unconstitutional?"

"I don't know, but they do it. So I guess I better say that graduation is a turning point, something about remembering these years for the rest of my life. Junk like that."

"Hey . . ." I was getting an idea. "Do you give your speech before or after we get our diplomas?"

"Right before. I speak and then we get them."

"Listen. Could you put something in your speech like . . ." I thought for a few seconds. "Like 'Although we're graduating today, we'll always be Claverfordians.' Um . . . 'Body and soul' maybe. 'Forever' maybe."

"I guess so." She closed her eyes. "'Claverford has marked us. We are hers forever.'"

"That's too . . . poetic. Could you say this exactly: 'Though we get our diplomas today, we will always be Claverfordians'?"

"It's important?"

I nodded. Maybe I could fool the spell into thinking

I would be at Claverford forever and everybody else would be too.

"'Though we receive our diplomas today, we will always be Claverfordians.' Is that it?"

"Perfect." But would it work?

Chapter Twenty

One more week.

Nothing much happened during finals week except finals. Occasionally somebody mentioned Grad Night, but then the conversation always went back to tests and flunking tests and parents going crazy.

I studied and worried about the end of the spell and looked forward to Grad Night all at the same time. I could concentrate on math and wonder about the solution to my life—my future after graduation. I sent mental petitions to the old lady. See how hard I'm studying? Don't I deserve to stay popular?

I was nice to Maud. I went to the store for Mom. See? I do good turns for lots of people. Can't I keep my wish? Please.

In language arts on Wednesday, I told Jared about meeting at Ardis's to go to Grad Night.

He said, "Okay, but I don't like Carlos."

"Me neither."

There were no classes on Friday, only a few leftover exams. My last test ended at noon. Afterward, I cleaned out my locker. I imagined leaving Jared's caricature behind to stun and terrify some new sixth grader, but in the end I took it.

The halls were empty. I walked all over the school. I was probably the only kid in world history who didn't want to graduate.

☀ ☀ ☀

Ardis had told us to come to her house at four thirty to get ready. The boys were coming at six, and Ardis's mother was going to give us dinner before we left at seven.

A pile of shoes sat on newspapers outside the door of Ardis's apartment. I rang the bell, and Ardis and Nina opened the door while I was untying my sneakers.

"Hi. Come on in," Ardis said.

"Any dust or grime on your body?" Nina said. "The disinfecting room is to your left."

It was like being in a department-store showroom. I smelled furniture polish, and everything was so clean, it almost sparkled, the way bathrooms do in TV commercials.

BeeBee was waiting for us in Ardis's bedroom.

Ardis lived in it, I guess, but it was *not* a kid's room. She slept in a four-poster bed with a canopy. Her desk and dresser were made of reddish wood with shiny brass handles and tapering legs. On the walls were framed oil paintings of landscapes and ocean scenes.

"Someday I'm going to sleep on a normal bed," Ardis said, "and have furniture that was built after Mesopotamia." She giggled. "Whenever that was."

"Can I see your dress?" BeeBee asked me. She was sitting at Ardis's dressing table, wearing a slip, a towel draped around her shoulders.

I took the dress out of its garment bag.

"Cool," Nina said. "Points."

It was something to get a compliment from Nina.

"Where are your dresses?" I asked.

They were hanging in Ardis's closet. I recognized Ardis's because she'd told me it was an African print. It only had one strap.

"How does the strap work?" I asked.

"You'll see," Ardis said.

"I love that strap," BeeBee said.

BeeBee's dress was apricot color, silk, with a vee neck. Nina's was beige lace over a pale-blue satiny sheath. "A hundred doilies died to make this," she said, touching the lace.

"Okay, guys," BeeBee said. "I'm ready for you."

"BeeBee's unbelievable," Ardis told me. "We should have before and after pictures."

BeeBee put shadows across Nina's cheeks and rubbed them in. Suddenly Nina had high cheekbones, and her broad face looked exotic, almost beautiful. Then BeeBee combed Nina's hair all on one side, hiding half of the left side of her face.

"Thanks," Nina said, staring at herself in the mirror. "I would have killed to look like this, and now I look like this."

Then it was Ardis's turn, and BeeBee shook her head. "You don't need me."

"My nose."

"Your nose fits your face." She brushed blush onto Ardis's cheeks. "A little mascara and you're done."

I was next.

"Your eyes are gorgeous," BeeBee said, applying eye shadow.

"They're brown," I said.

"She knows they're brown," Nina said, pulling the sheath part of her dress over her head. "You think a blind person is doing your makeup?"

"Brown's a good warm color," BeeBee said. "And half the world wants lashes like yours."

BeeBee did my hair too. She pulled it tight to the top of my head, and then left the ends flopping. It looked like something out of a magazine, and she showed me how to do it, so I could wear it that way whenever I wanted, which would be always. Putting my hair up didn't turn me into a swan, but I wasn't a no-neck owl anymore either. Ardis lent me a wooden comb with inlaid mother-of-pearl, which made my hair look dressy as well as fabulous.

BeeBee didn't spend half as much time on herself as she spent on us. "Only plastic surgery would work for me." She put the cover back on her lipstick. "Add a forehead. Add a chin." She sounded perfectly cheerful.

Ardis saw my expression. "Don't worry. BeeBee likes the way she looks."

"If you're pretty," BeeBee said, taking her dress off its hanger, "your self-portraits aren't interesting."

In an astonishing act of generosity, Maud had let me wear the pearls she got from Grandma for Christmas. I fastened them around my neck, over my old locket.

Nina was struggling with her zipper. "I wanted to lose five pounds for Grad Night, but I gained six."

"Points off," I said, feeling daring, "for putting yourself down." I hadn't teased any of them before.

"Wilma got you," BeeBee said. She was the first one dressed. "How do I look?"

"Do you have a necklace?" Ardis asked.

BeeBee looked at herself in Ardis's huge oval mirror. "It needs something, right?"

"Let me see what I have." Ardis took a jewelry box out of the top drawer of her bureau.

We all looked. Everything was big and heavy. Big jewelry was right for Ardis, but BeeBee needed something delicate.

"I looked okay when I tried it on at home," she said. "Some artist I am. I should have noticed."

My locket might look good. I didn't need it because of Maud's pearls. But maybe it was too plain. "You can wear this if you want to." I fumbled at the clasp. "It's just an ordinary heart. . . ."

BeeBee fastened the chain around her neck. It worked. It was simple, like her dress.

"That's it," Ardis said. "It's perfect."

"And if you get lonely for my dog or my mom, you can look inside."

BeeBee laughed. "Thanks, Wilma. I'm glad you're—"

The doorbell rang. The sound was muffled by the acres of carpet between the door and Ardis's bedroom.

"Dad will get it, but we better hurry," Ardis said. She put on big gold hoop earrings.

I stepped into my dress, zipped up the back and stood in front of the mirror.

I was pretty! I never was before, at least not that I could see. But now I was. Whatever BeeBee had done to my eyes, they were huge, and—I don't know—appealing. And in this dress—unlike in my Claverford uniform—I had a visible waist and breasts and hips, all of them proportioned about right. I did not look like a beaver tonight.

"I guess I'm done," Nina said.

"Me too." Ardis joined me in front of the mirror and held out her arms to Nina and BeeBee. "Come here."

The doorbell rang again. We crowded next to Ardis and faced ourselves in the mirror. I looked like I belonged in the reflection with the three other girls.

"We're knockouts," Nina said.

The doorbell rang again.

"I wish I'd brought my camera," BeeBee said.

"I have one," Ardis said.

"You can't take the picture," Nina said. "You have to be in it."

"I'll get Shanara."

While we waited, the doorbell rang one more time. The four of them had arrived. BeeBee made a final adjustment to Nina's hair. "Try not to move your head too much."

"Yeah, right."

Shanara was about nine years old. "You need me, so now I'm allowed in here," she said. "Where's the camera?"

Ardis gave it to her, and we assembled in front of the mirror again. Shanara stood next to it.

"Smile."

We already were. She snapped.

Chapter Twenty-one

The four boys stood up when we came into the living room. They had been sitting on the couch, in a row like eggs on a refrigerator door. Ardis's father stood across from them, leaning on the back of a chair.

Jared was wearing a gray suit, a maroon shirt, and a yellow tie. The tie was just like him—surprising in a nice way. He smiled at me. I smiled back, glad he was the one I was going with.

Carlos whistled. His eyes traveled across all of us but lingered an extra second on me.

"I believe Mrs. Lundy has laid some food out in the dining room," Mr. Lundy said.

We ate quickly. Nobody said much. Five minutes ago we were having fun getting ready, and now—nothing.

"What do you think Mr. Winby will wear?" Ardis said finally.

The teachers and Mr. Winby always came to Grad Night in costume.

"A lion suit," Jared said. "My brother says he does it every year. He has an authority complex."

"I hear Ms. Hannah's coming as Ophelia," BeeBee said.

They started talking about what costumes some teachers would wear and what others should wear. I watched Jared. He was laughing at something Ardis's boyfriend, Russ, had said. Jared was the friendliest-looking of the boys, the nicest, the kindest, the best kisser, I'd bet, the most fun, everything.

My last night. I was going to have a fabulous time. With Jared. With all of them.

In the elevator down from Ardis's apartment, I stood between Jared and Carlos. Jared moved closer to me. So did Carlos. This might be the last time Carlos would have anything to do with me. I wouldn't miss him much.

It was warm out. Russ and Ardis were dancing as they walked. Liam was laughing at something Nina had whispered to him. BeeBee and Carlos bumped their hips into each other as they walked, making them zigzag across the sidewalk.

Jared and I held hands. I felt shy.

"I may be better at zoos than dances," Jared said.

He was feeling the same way as me. That made me more comfortable. "Could Twentieth Street be a kissing zone?" I asked.

"It is," he said, grinning. "I saw a sign."

He kissed me. Somebody whistled. Somebody clapped. Nina said, "Points. Many points." BeeBee said, "Keep it up. No breathing."

When he let me go, I said, "Everybody has to kiss on Twentieth Street."

Liam kissed Nina on the lips—but quickly. Ardis and Russ got into it, though. I stamped my feet and clapped till my palms tingled.

"Come on, lover." BeeBee threw her arms around Carlos. They kissed. BeeBee's eyes were closed. But Carlos's were open. Over her shoulder, he looked at me.

"I hate that guy," Jared muttered.

Grad Night was in the basement of Claverford, in the gym. We heard the band as soon as we opened the door to the stairs. Downstairs, we walked along the corridor. Teachers' lounge on the left. Coach's office on the right. Girls' bathroom on the right. I'd probably never be through here again.

We followed a stream of kids. The band was loud,

but the sound was mixed with kids' voices, laughing, yelling to each other.

Mr. Winby in his lion suit prowled through the crowd, roaring and then laughing.

The air-conditioned air was chilly, although it still smelled of sweat and sneakers. The Grad Night committee had tried to make the gym look like a nightclub. The fluorescent lights were draped with blue cloth that dimmed their glare. Near the long table with soda and pretzels and potato chips were smaller tables covered with blue paper tablecloths. In the middle of each table was a flashlight standing on end, pointing its light at the ceiling.

Ms. Hannah, as Ophelia in a floor-length dress and carrying a bouquet, stood behind the long table talking to a man with a green face who held a beaker of purple liquid. It was Mr. Pike, as a science experiment gone wrong.

The band played under one of the basketball hoops. Somehow a ball was suspended in the hoop so it looked like it was going to crash down on the keyboard player's head, but it never did.

The last dance I'd been to was the Spring Dance in March. I hadn't danced once. I don't know why I went, except I hoped it would be different for a change. It was why I'd gone to every other dance before this, and not one had ever been different.

Tonight was different.

I love to dance. I'm not graceful, but I have lots of energy. I hadn't been dancing for more than a minute before I noticed that kids were imitating me. They were doing The Wilma.

If only I could bottle tonight and take a sip of it every so often for the rest of my life.

After the next dance, I had to go to the bathroom. On my way out of the gym, kids kept pulling me in to dance with them, so it took me a song and a half to leave, dancing all the way.

Somebody was in a stall, crying.

"Hello? Are you okay?" I asked.

"Yeah. Go away."

"Daphne?"

"Wilma?"

I could guess what was wrong. She was being left out. Nobody was dancing with her. Nobody was paying any attention to her. She could have been me a month ago.

"Do you want to go back in with me?"

She was quiet for a minute. "Okay."

It struck me—suppose it *had* been a month ago. If

I'd gone into the bathroom then and Daphne had been crying, I never would have asked her to go in with me. I wouldn't have wanted her unpopularity to rub off on me, even though I was unpopular too. But now that I was popular, I wanted to help her. Well, when—and if—the spell ended, I would still be Daphne's friend if she wanted me to be. I'd learned that much, anyway.

Daphne came out. Her eyes were red and a bit puffy, but not too bad.

"You look great," she told me.

"You do too." But she didn't. Her green dress made her look even more washed-out than usual. And she'd done something to her hair to try to make it less stringy, but it only looked messy. She looked in the mirror and didn't answer.

"Ready?" I asked.

She nodded.

In the gym, the band was playing a reggae number. Jared was at the food table. He saw me and headed my way. We started dancing, and I pulled Daphne in to join us.

She could dance! She got totally into the music and flowed, like a snake. Her long hands, her arms, all of her pulsed rhythmically. I should have expected it, from the slinky way she skated. Other kids noticed, looked startled, and started imitating her instead of me.

So here we were, the three ex-loners—Jared, Daphne, and me—dancing our feet off, the envy of everyone. I grinned at them, and they grinned back.

If only it could last.

After another dance, Daphne, Jared, and I took a break and got some food. We sat at one of the little tables.

"I never heard of a nightclub lit by flashlights," I said, clicking ours on and off. "They should be candles, but probably Mr. Winby was afraid of fire, so he got flashlights."

Ardis and Russ pulled chairs over and joined us. Russ put his hand over the flashlight. His fingers glowed pink-red.

The band stopped playing, and Mr. Winby took the guitarist's microphone. "Roar," he yelled into it. There was feedback, and his roar turned into a screech.

Liam, Nina, and Carlos dragged chairs to our table. BeeBee sat on the floor, leaning against Carlos's legs.

"Listen up, kids. While the band takes a well-deserved break from the evil noise it produces so professionally—"

Somebody yelled, "Get hip, Mr. Winby."

"—our talented faculty will perform a little skit for you." He bowed and put back the mike.

Mr. Pike entered the circle of light around the basketball hoop. He carried a pointer, which he tried to stick in his ear. "Maybe this will get the wax out," he said, rocking back and forth while he spoke. "It's long enough."

It was a perfect imitation of himself, except that he was rocking much faster than usual, and his ordinary ear-picking weapon was a bent paper clip.

"Pardon me." Ms. Hannah in her Ophelia outfit joined him. "Wherefore you are as eminent a scientist as the bard was a poet, you will have no trouble inventing . . ."

Ardis took my hand. Everybody was holding hands, all over the gym.

More teachers joined the skit, till they were all there. At the end, Mr. Winby said, "Please notice that these talented performers made fun of themselves, not of you, although they were sorely tempted. I think they deserve a round of applause, don't you?"

We let go of each other's hands to clap. Then he had us clap for the Grad Night committee. And then he told us that the band would play three final numbers and Grad Night would end.

The last dance was a real oldie, "Sixteen Candles," a slow number. We didn't do it as couples. All nine of us

(I pulled Daphne in) got into a group hug and swayed together.

I made myself not think about graduation. I was part of a family, and they loved me and cared about me. And if I could, I'd stay here, hugging and being hugged forever.

I wormed myself as far into the hug as I could to get maximum squeezing. And they hugged me extra hard because I was their favorite. Then the song ended and Grad Night was over. And tears rolled down my face.

Chapter Twenty-two

I couldn't sleep. I didn't want to sleep. I'd never have another night like tonight. Tomorrow would come, and then Sunday and then Monday morning, and it would almost certainly be finished. *I* would be finished. And there was nothing I could do about it.

I'd miss being popular. I'd miss being *magically* popular, so that every single kid liked me. I'd miss feeling safe to be myself, more myself than I'd ever been when I was worrying what people would think of me. But what I'd miss most were my friends—Jared, Ardis, Daphne, Nina, and BeeBee. They felt like real friends, not magic-spell friends.

I had to talk to them. But if I talked to them before graduation, it wouldn't do any good. They'd say they liked me and they'd like me forever. They'd swear it. And after graduation, they wouldn't talk to me.

Well, I'd make them. I couldn't make them like me

after graduation, but at least I should be able to get them to talk to me.

Monday afternoon would be my only chance, before everyone left for camp or vacation or relatives. I'd get them all together. Except Jared. I'd talk to him alone.

✦ ✦ ✦

I called Ardis first.

"Could you come over to my house Monday afternoon?" I began. "Although you might not want to."

"Why not?"

"I don't know—you may have other things you need to do . . ." I trailed off.

"Will Reggie be there?"

"Sure."

"Then I'll come."

"Great! It means a lot to me. Ardis . . ."

"What?"

"Do you promise? You'll come, even if you don't want to?"

"What's going on, Wilma? I said I'd come."

"I know. It's just that there's something important I have to tell you, only I can't tell it yet. I'm inviting Ni—"

"Why can't you tell now?"

"Because I can't. You'll see." If the spell didn't end,

I'd make up something to say. "Do you promise?"

"Yes, I promise."

"For sure?"

"Wilma! When have I ever broken a promise?"

"You never promised me anything before."

"Oh. Well, I never break a promise. I'll be there."

After Ardis, I called everybody else, and they all promised to come, although Nina took points off for making her promise. Now I just had to cross my fingers and toes that the promises would hold.

I didn't call Jared. I was going to catch him right after graduation. I had the most hope that he'd go on liking me, but if he didn't, I wasn't going to beg him. The others I was willing to beg, but not Jared.

❀   ❀   ❀

Monday. Doomsday. I couldn't eat breakfast. Mom asked if I was sick, but I said I was only nervous.

Maud said, "It's just middle school, Wilma. It's not the Nobel Prize for veterinary medicine."

My face was blotchy. My Claverford uniform was rumpled. I tried to put my hair up the way BeeBee had done it, but it kept coming out lopsided. For three weeks it hadn't mattered how I looked. Today it mattered, and today I looked lousy.

When the elevator door opened, Suzanne and her parents were inside.

"Wilma!" Suzanne squealed. "You look super!"

Outside, it was raining. Suzanne buzzed on and on. I looked at my watch—ten after eight.

It was almost impossible to do the ordinary stuff— walk, breathe, try not to listen to Suzanne. When we got to the subway, I looked for the old lady. The train came. No old lady. Fiftieth Street. Forty-second. Thirty-fourth. Twenty-eighth. Twenty-third. Our stop. No old lady.

By the time we got out of the station, the rain had stopped. It was the same weather as the day I got my wish.

And then we were there. We turned into the entrance. Could the transformation happen as soon as I stepped inside, ending exactly the way it had begun? I stopped outside the doorway so suddenly that the person behind me crashed into me.

"Sorry," I muttered.

"Anytime." It was Timothy.

"What's the matter with you?" Maud said.

"Nothing." I took a deep, shaky breath and stepped inside.

Chapter Twenty-three

BeeBee was in the lobby with her mother. She grinned and waved to me. The end hadn't come . . . yet.

Mom and Maud and I followed people up the stairs to the auditorium. What goes up doesn't always come down. The Wilma who was going up, the popular one, might not come down.

Seventh graders handed programs to everybody as we filed into the auditorium. I had to sit in front with the other eighth graders. We were in alphabetical order, and I was between Ovideo Stout and Erica Talbot.

When everybody had come in, we all had to stand to sing "The Star-Spangled Banner." I just moved my lips. My mouth was too dry to sing.

When we finished, Mr. Winby gave a speech. I didn't hear a word. I wanted to climb over everybody's legs and run up the aisle, yelling, Stop! No graduation!

After Mr. Winby was done, Mr. Imber, the music

teacher, played the piano. Even though the auditorium was air-conditioned, sweat beads formed on my forehead and my blouse was soaked—and I was shivering.

The next event on the program was giving certificates to the honors students. I was one of them, so I would have to go onstage. I wasn't sure I'd be able to stand up.

I managed it, although I was puffing by the time I got to the stage, convinced I'd left a wet trail from my perspiration. There had been applause for the other kids, but when Ms. Virrone, the assistant principal, gave me my certificate, the clapping from the first four rows was deafening.

After the honors awards, Daphne got up to give her valedictory speech. She was the only hope I had left, and I didn't have much hope. But I clapped hard when she climbed onstage, and the applause, which was weak at the beginning, got stronger.

Daphne began her speech by remembering how it had felt three years ago to be a sixth grader and how exciting it had been to have left elementary school behind. She went on to say that it was exciting yet again to move on to high school. She said we had to start thinking about what we were going to make ourselves into. We had to look out at the world and see where we would fit in it someday and how we would do—and she meant more than what we would be when we grew up.

Then she said, "We're different from the sixth graders who arrived three years ago. I know I am. But even though I've learned a lot and am a better person for it, most of my years here were not happy. For most of them I was without friends. And then, a few weeks ago, a friend found me. I'm saying this—"

She was talking about me! I was surprised—overwhelmed—and I missed what she said next. Then I heard ". . . friends we make during our teen years can stay with us forever, if we're lucky. And friendship is more than hanging out; sometimes friendship is picking your friend up when she's down or has been stepped on; sometimes it's bringing your friend into the same circle with your other friends; and sometimes it *is* just hanging out.

"But whatever it is, it's because of our friends that we are never really going to graduate from Claverford. In our hearts—in the truest sense—even though we get our diplomas today, we will always be Claverfordians, remaining forever in eighth grade in the company of the people we care for the most."

That was the end. I clapped as hard as I could, and the applause grew again. It might be the last time I'd be able to help her out.

But maybe her speech had worked. Maybe staying in the eighth grade in our hearts would be enough for the old lady.

Mr. Imber started playing the piano again. The eighth graders, including me, marched up the right-hand aisle, behind the last row of seats, and into the left-hand aisle. This was it.

"And now," Mr. Winby said, "the moment some of you have been waiting for since you came here three years ago. Camilla Abrams, you're first. Come on up."

Camilla climbed the steps to the stage and walked behind Mr. Winby to stand on his left.

"Congratulations." He handed her the rolled-up diploma tied with a ribbon. She took it.

And nothing happened, as far as I could tell. She shook Mr. Winby's hand and left the stage.

Nothing special happened with the next kid either. Or the next.

The first of the kids I knew best to get her diploma was Nina (Draper). Maybe she'd look at me so I could figure out what was going on. She did. As she walked up the aisle, she looked for her friends, and she grinned at me. She grinned at me! She was still my friend. One down. Many more to go.

When Jared got his diploma, he waved it at me and

grinned. I loved his grin. I loved that it was aimed at me. Still aimed at me.

Ardis got her diploma, and then BeeBee did, and then Suzanne. As she left the stage, Suzanne held it over her head, like an Olympic medal. And as she walked up the aisle, she smiled at all the most popular kids—including me!

Then it was my turn. Maybe the old lady was waiting for me to get my diploma. I made it to the stage. I was supposed to accept the diploma with my left hand and shake Mr. Winby's hand with my right. I did it backward. When I held the diploma, I couldn't tell if anything had happened. I felt like I was having a stroke, but that might have been from panic, not from something really happening.

I tripped on the first step down from the stage. I heard people gasp, but I caught myself and didn't fall. When I joined the kids waiting halfway up the aisle, Ovideo asked me if I was all right, and Ardis smiled sympathetically at me.

So it wasn't over yet. It was still going on. Maybe Daphne's speech had worked, after all.

Parents and students milled around in the lobby after the ceremony. I couldn't find Jared—but it was wonderful to know that I didn't *need* to find him. Mom and Maud and I headed for the door with Ardis and her family.

"We should do something when we leave the building," I told Ardis. "Something to commemorate our final exit." My heart was thudding again. This could be it. It could have waited till now to end.

"That sounds like we're dying."

One of us might be.

"What if we step across the threshold facing each other," I said. "So we can see each other take the step into the future." So I could see Ardis's expression change, if *it* happened.

"So I can say at our fiftieth reunion . . ."

We were almost at the door. We were at the door.

"Now," I said.

We faced each other and stepped across.

Chapter Twenty-four

$\mathcal{N}$othing happened.

"An eighth-grade Wilma and a one-second-old ex-eighth-grade Wilma look the same," Ardis reported.

The spell was still on! I would stay popular! I would keep my friends! *Thank you, old lady!*

"Maybe you do look different," Ardis said.

My heart stopped.

"Happier," she added.

It started again.

Ardis's father called her. So she left me, saying she'd be over at three.

"What a great graduation!" I said to Mom and Maud. "I wish Reggie could have seen it." I hugged Mom. "Wasn't it a great graduation?" I hugged Maud. "Wasn't it?"

"I guess." Maud straightened her blouse. "The

valedictorian's speech wasn't bad."

It was wonderful not to have a big secret. Not to have one to reveal, that is. Now I just had to think of a good reason for having invited everyone over.

Mom took us to my favorite restaurant for lunch. It's Middle Eastern, small and cozy. The food was better than ever before. The waiters were friendlier. Even Maud was all right, although she asked me twice why I was grinning like an idiot.

Mom and Maud didn't go home with me. Mom had to go to work, and Maud was going to her best friend Portia's house.

At home I changed into shorts and a T-shirt as I thought about what my fake big secret could be.

Nothing was new with Reggie. We weren't moving. Mom hadn't lost her job. Maud hadn't run away from home. What if I said I wanted to plan what we were going to do together at Elliot next year? That might work.

At ten to three, I dumped a package of chocolate-chip cookies into a bowl and took them into my room. At five to three, Daphne came, and the rest of them came about a minute later.

In the bedroom, Nina flopped across Maud's bed. "BeeBee thinks you're going to say that your mom's getting married ag—"

"I do not think that!"

She plowed on. "Ardis thinks Reggie's going to be a father, and I think you're skipping Elliot and going straight to veterinary school."

I laughed. "Nope. None of the above. Have a cookie." I handed the bowl to Ardis, who was sitting cross-legged on my bed. She took one and passed the bowl to BeeBee. Daphne was sitting at Maud's desk, not looking as comfortable as the rest of them. I stood next to her and looked at the four of them.

"If I could have tryouts for friends," I said, "among everybody in the world, I would pick you guys."

"Points off for senti—"

BeeBee choked on her cookie. "Water," she gasped, coughing.

"CPR—" Ardis said.

I raced for the kitchen, calling over my shoulder, "CPR's only when you're not breathing."

I ran water. I could hear BeeBee coughing over the sound of the tap. I filled a glass and turned away from the sink.

The old lady was sitting at the kitchen table.

I dropped the glass. It shattered.

"Reggie could cut his paw," I said automatically. "I have to clean up."

"He won't come in, Wilma," she said in her rich voice.

He didn't. And I didn't hear BeeBee coughing anymore, either.

"Thanks for the wish. And thanks for not taking it away."

"That's why I'm here. It must end now."

"Why? Why does it have to end? I wished to be popular."

"At Claverford. You graduated today."

"But I didn't mean that part of it. You knew what I meant."

"I did indeed." She sighed. "People are rarely wise in their wishes."

"Can't you give me what I want? Please?"

She shook her head. "I could only give you your wish exactly as you wished it."

"Could you give me another—"

"Hush." She closed her eyes. I tried to talk, tried to tell her what Daphne had said in her speech, but I couldn't. I couldn't move my lips. She opened her eyes. "It's over now, Wilma. You are as you were before."

Reggie howled.

I turned at the sound. I turned back. On the kitchen table was the glass filled with water, unbroken. I heard BeeBee coughing in my room. And the old lady was gone.

Chapter Twenty-five

I stared at the glass. I didn't want to leave the kitchen.

Nina yelled, "Hurry, Wilma, you jerk."

Jerk! She wouldn't have called me that ten minutes ago.

Ardis rushed in. "Give me that." She glared at me, took the glass, and left.

I followed her. She handed the glass to BeeBee. They were crowded around her. BeeBee sipped the water and gradually stopped coughing. She stared at me over the rim of the glass.

They were all looking at me. I saw the realization go through them that something was different. Nina frowned, shook her head, and frowned again. BeeBee's mouth hung open. She held the glass tilted. She was going to spill water on her jeans. Daphne half smiled at me, looking confused.

Ardis's face was dark red. She looked furious, so

mad she was fighting back tears.

They didn't think I was wonderful anymore. They weren't my friends anymore. I fought back tears too.

I took the glass from BeeBee.

"Tha—" She trailed off.

"What just happened?" Ardis asked. "What did you do, Wilma?"

If I tried to talk, I was going to cry. It wouldn't be good to cry in front of people who didn't like me. I started crying anyway. Tears oozed out and then a flood came. Reggie rushed to me, wagging his tail. I petted him and went on crying. "Sorry," I got out.

Daphne came over and patted my shoulder. Nobody else moved.

I wanted to go on crying now that I'd started. When I stopped, I was going to have to tell them something, and I didn't know what to say. I never should have invited them. I should have just let it happen and faced them in the fall. They hadn't liked me before the wish. It hadn't killed me.

But I finally stopped crying. I looked up.

"What happened?" BeeBee said. "Something happened."

"Wilma did something," Ardis said. "I don't know what."

"And then she cried," Nina added, "so we'd feel sorry for her."

"I didn't do anything." I couldn't tell them. They didn't like me anymore, and telling a crazy story, even though it was true, wouldn't make any difference.

Ardis said, "If you're not going to tell us, I have to go. I have to pack for camp."

BeeBee stood up. Ardis and Nina turned toward the door. Daphne stayed where she was, standing uncertainly in the middle of the room.

"Oh, I almost forgot." BeeBee reached into a pocket and pulled out a small packet wrapped in tissue paper. She handed it to me. "It's your locket."

Ardis started to leave.

I couldn't let them go. "Wait!"

They turned.

"I still have Ardis's comb." I went to my bureau. I was just stalling. What was I going to do?

"Talk," Daphne urged. "Tell them something. Anything."

I handed the comb to Ardis. "Thanks." Then I took a deep breath. "Remember May twenty-sixth? A Tuesday? That was the day I became popular. . . ."

BeeBee came back and sat on my bed. Ardis and Nina stood by the door. Daphne sat next to BeeBee. I stood between my desk and Maud's. And I told them.

Daphne listened the way you'd listen to a friend, nodding, smiling, frowning in all the right places. BeeBee said "far out" once, and "oh, wow" once, but mostly she fiddled with her hair, winding a strand around her finger and unwinding it. Nina crossed her arms and stared at me without saying anything. Ardis made clicking noises with her tongue every so often, like everything I said was garbage. She never looked at me, just stared up at the ceiling.

When I finished, Daphne said, "Something happened. I agree. Right here." She gestured at the room. "But magic? The end of a wish?"

I could see she wanted to believe me, and if she didn't, even though she wanted to, I had no chance with the rest of them.

"It's what happened," I said. "I wasn't popular before, and after Ms. Hannah read my essay, I was unpopular. What could make me suddenly popular? So popular that everybody liked me?"

BeeBee said, "How should we know?"

"Points for imagination, Wilma."

Daphne said, "What if the food in the cafeteria was drugged?"

"Yeah," BeeBee said. "I like that."

"What drug would make everybody like me? Only me?"

"I don't know," Nina said. "But—"

"Listen. Here's proof. Remember when we went skating with Stephanie? She didn't like me."

"And you made her upset," BeeBee said.

"We should have realized then that you were a creep," Nina said.

"I got mad when she didn't like me. But I told her I was sorry."

"That's not good enough," Nina said. "Saying you're sorry isn't good enough."

"Why does that prove there was a spell?" Daphne asked.

"Because she's the only one who was immune to me. Because she didn't go to Claverford. She wasn't under the spell."

"But," Daphne said, "I like you now. Am I bewitched now?"

"No. The spell ended. You're not bewitched. You really like me."

"I believe it," Ardis said.

"You do?" BeeBee asked. "You think?"

"Yeah, I do. It felt like the end of a spell would feel, like I had been sitting on cushions a mile high, and they disappeared, and I landed on a pile of sharp rocks."

Nina nodded. "Maybe. It was too sudden to be normal."

"A spell?" BeeBee said. "For real?"

"Tell us, Wilma," Ardis's voice was extra soft, extra polite, "why did you wait for it to end to let us know? It would have been nice to know I *had* to like you."

"You wouldn't have believed me, and anyway, I wasn't sure it was going to end."

"So if it didn't end, you would have gone on fooling us. You don't know how it felt when you walked into the room before. It was . . ." Ardis stopped. "Forget it."

"What was it like?" BeeBee asked. "Maybe it was different for me because I was coughing."

"It was like I had this stuffed animal . . ." Ardis looked at Reggie and almost smiled. "No. It was like I had this pet. It loved me no matter what, and I loved it no matter what. And then it came into the room, and it wasn't my pet anymore. It had turned into something else, an animal that didn't like me—"

"I still like you."

She ignored me. "—a horse maybe. Not a horse. I

don't know what. A fish maybe. It doesn't matter what. It wasn't my pet, and it didn't like me and I didn't like it."

"I still like you," I repeated.

"That's not the way it was for me," BeeBee said. "I mean, I was coughing, so it happened slower, not as dramatic. I drank the water and looked at her and I thought, 'Oh, it's Wilma. Why did I think she was so special?'" She looked at me. "Sorry. It's just what I thought."

How was I going to break through that?

"What was it like for you?" Daphne asked Nina.

"First I was stunned. After BeeBee stopped choking to death, I mean. Then I thought, 'Points off, Nina. Many points off for letting Wilma Sturtz make a fool of you.'"

Ardis said, "Remember when I came to see your caricature and Suzanne barged in? Then, when she left, I said I was surprised she liked the drawing, and you said she couldn't harm you. That was because of the spell, wasn't it?"

I didn't answer. What could I say? She knew the answer. But I never once thought I was hurting anyone.

Ardis turned to Nina and BeeBee and Daphne.

"She said Suzanne couldn't harm her because *I* was her protection. And I felt great about that. But she was lying."

Nina nodded. "She's been lying all along." She faced me. "Is that what you brought us over for? To tell us about the spell after it ended? Well, you told us. Can we go now?"

"She invited us because she wants to keep us as friends," Daphne said.

"No," Nina said. "She invited us because she wants to stay popular."

"I didn't. I—"

"Then why did she invite me?" Daphne interrupted. "I can't keep her popular."

"I invited you because I *like* you. All of you. Listen. Believe me." They had to believe me. "I wasn't any different when I was under the spell than I am now. I didn't *have* to be different. I could be the same old Wilma and everyone would like me anyway."

"Maybe," Ardis said, "but you don't seem the same. Maybe I can't remember what happened during the spell accurately."

"Maybe you've been bewitched not to like her now," Daphne said. "Maybe you were bewitched a long time ago not to like me." She giggled. "Maybe it's *all* a spell.

It doesn't matter what kind of a person you are. An old lady just decides whether you're popular or not, and Wilma's the only one to catch her at it."

"Far out," BeeBee said.

They all stared at Daphne, me included.

She went on. "Anyway, Wilma seems different now to me too. The popularity glow is gone, I guess. But she *is* the same person. And if you don't see that, you're going to miss out."

Daphne made me feel like crying all over again.

"Maybe you're right," Ardis said. "Maybe she *is* the same person. But she seems different. I don't know her anymore."

BeeBee and Nina nodded.

"But you do know me. You've known me all along." I wanted to scream, to wail, *I like you. Like me back. Please like me.* "Ardis, didn't I help you stop being so afraid of dogs? Didn't I help you with history?"

"Thank you very much," she snapped.

I didn't mean she had to be grateful. But what did I mean? After all, why should they like me? I had had fun with them, but they'd had fun with a person they'd *had* to like.

"Can we go now?" Nina said.

Chapter Twenty-Six

BeeBee stood up.

"No. Wait," I said. "Remember what I said before BeeBee started choking—that I'd pick you for friends out of everybody in the world. Being popular was wonderful, but having you as friends was the best part."

Nina rolled her eyes, but BeeBee nodded. "We had fun at my sleepover. I couldn't believe you brought your dog with you."

"The thing is, if I met the old lady tomorrow, I wouldn't ask to be popular again, I'd ask for us to go on being friends." I'd finally said it. I'd finally told them what mattered to me now: not being popular, but being friends with them. Now they'd understand. It was true.

"You'd do it again," Ardis said. "You don't get it."

"What? Do what again?"

"You'd still wish for us to be *forced* to like you."

Oh.

She was right. That *is* what I was saying. But they should have a choice about liking me or not. After all, I had a choice about them.

"You don't need magic for me," Daphne said.

"Before today," Ardis said, "if somebody had asked me my name, I'd have said, 'Ardis Lundy and I like Wilma Sturtz.'" She sat down on my bed. "Now I don't know. I mean, I think we had fun together, but I'm not sure anymore. Yesterday, you felt like one of my lungs, but now, the friendship seems like an illusion."

"It's not an illusion on my side. I wasn't pretending."

"She didn't have to pretend," Daphne said. "You had to like her anyway, even if she was mean."

Ardis smoothed out a wrinkle in my comforter and didn't say anything.

"And why would she pretend to be *my* friend?" Daphne added.

"I keep thinking about you," Ardis said, nodding. "And about the caricature, and bringing Reggie to a sleepover, which nobody would do if they were faking to get in with us. And I get mixed up."

"I was being myself, spell or no spell," I said. "Look, Ardis, I liked you before the spell. You were nice to me after Ms. Hannah—"

Reggie started barking, and then the doorbell rang. I went to get it, closing the bedroom door behind me. Stay till we finish talking. Please stay.

I opened the door. Suzanne stood in the hall.

Chapter Twenty-seven

As soon as she saw me, Suzanne started laughing. "I was right!" she gasped between howls. "I felt something. . . . We were at my aunt's. . . . I said I wasn't feeling . . . I had to see . . . You're not . . . anymore . . . You're back . . ."

I heard my bedroom door open. Reggie bounded to Suzanne, wagging his tail.

She gave a final peal of laughter. "You are going to be so sorry you said I wet my bed. The anus story will be . . ."

Thank heavens I was me and not Suzanne. Even if I had no friends at all. But I didn't have no friends, I had Reggie and Daphne—and maybe Jared.

There were footsteps behind me.

"And the bed-wetting story will be too!" It was Daphne's voice.

I turned. Ardis and Daphne were there.

"Hi, Suzanne," Ardis said.

Suzanne looked at Ardis, looked at me. I could read her thoughts. Is Wilma still popular? No, she couldn't be. Then why is Ardis here?

"Hi, Ardis." She ignored Daphne. "Did you come because . . . because Wilma, um, reverted?"

"What do you mean?" Ardis said. "Nothing happened to Wilma."

What?

"We were just hanging out."

"Oh." Suzanne thought about it. "Well, I'm not busy right now. I could hang out too."

Daphne said, "Who invited you?"

"You came at a bad time," Ardis said. "Sorry. Shouldn't she go, Wilma? I mean, it's your house."

I nodded, grinning. "Another time, Suzanne. Maybe in fifty years."

"Okay. I'm going. But when you're through here, Ardis, come up to me. I want to tell you something fantastic." She turned to me. "Or you could come up when they leave, Wilma." She backed out. Reggie wagged his tail at her. I locked the door.

I turned to Ardis and Daphne. "Thanks."

We stood there in the foyer.

"I couldn't let Suzanne be nasty to you," Ardis said.

Then she led us back into my room.

BeeBee was sprawled across my bed. Nina was in Maud's chair.

"Suzanne's too much," BeeBee said, grinning. "She's a riot."

Suzanne just wants to be popular too, I thought, surprising myself.

"Look," I said, going back to our discussion, "it's not fair. If there hadn't been a spell, you wouldn't have gotten to know me, because you wouldn't have bothered, but—"

"Points off," Nina said. "Lots of people never get to know lots of people."

"It's not that simple," Daphne said, "and you know it."

"Right." I nodded. They had to know. Especially Ardis, once known as The Mountain, had to know. "Nobody has anything to do with somebody who isn't popular, and you can't be popular if nobody has anything to do with you."

"Catch twenty-two," Nina said.

I frowned at her. "You say, 'Catch twenty-two,' and then you don't think about it anymore because you said something smart. But it *is* that way."

BeeBee laughed. "She got you that time, Neen."

I wasn't finished. "Nobody has anything to do with anybody who isn't popular, even if they're really okay."

I swallowed. "Even if they're me."

"You were nice to me when we studied for the debate," BeeBee said, staring up at the ceiling. "And I wasn't nice back."

"I'm nice to kids who aren't popular," Ardis said.

"You wave," Daphne said. "You say hi. Big deal."

"Sometimes you do a little more," I said. "You talked to me after Ms. Hannah read my essay. But then you went back to waving."

Ardis shook her head. "This is so strange, Wilma. You're different, but the same. I can't get used to it."

"Are you going to try?" Daphne said. "Or are you going to walk away?"

Nobody said anything for a few seconds. I felt like a dress in a store window that the three of them were deciding whether or not to buy.

I waited. A car alarm went off outside. I was through pleading. It was up to them now.

"Promise not to trick us again," Ardis said.

"I can't trick you again. It's over."

"Points off for not answering. You can't be trusted," Nina said.

"I promise not to trick you again even if I could."

"I'll try," Ardis said. "I don't know. I guess I'll try." A grin started. "But don't give Reggie away."

It was the first time she'd joked since the spell ended. I felt such relief, I could hardly talk. "I won't," I got out.

"I'll try too," BeeBee said. "It was out of sight, being bewitched. It was subtle. I didn't feel anything or anything."

"Are you two a package deal?" Nina asked, nodding at Daphne.

"No," Daphne said.

"No," I added, "but we're friends. If I had a sleepover or a party, I'd invite her too."

"You're a great dancer," BeeBee told Daphne.

"Thank you."

Nobody said anything. I wanted to be sure of them, but I couldn't be. Without a spell, I couldn't be. The friendship would have to be their wish as well as mine. It would have to keep on being what each of us wanted, or it would end. Which was right, I supposed. Which was right, even if I wanted more certainty than that.

"I really have to go or my mom will put a spell on me," Ardis said. "I'm leaving for camp tomorrow."

"We're going to Europe," BeeBee said. "Dad's taking me to see Florence . . ."

Whoever that was.

". . . and Rome."

Oh, Italy.

"What train was the old lady on?" Nina asked. "What did she look like?"

"I could make Carlos my slave," BeeBee said.

"I could— Never mind," Daphne said.

"Well, I have to go," Ardis repeated. "I'll call you from camp. Can you put Reggie on the phone? Would he bark?"

"I'll train him," I said, smiling.

When everyone left, I stared at the door for a minute. It was over. But I wasn't the same as before it started. I knew four girls and one boy better than I had three weeks ago, and maybe I had four friends. And maybe one boyfriend.

I ran to call Jared. The answering machine picked up. While I left a message, I pictured him listening and not picking up because he didn't want to talk to me.

Chapter Twenty-eight

Mom brought home cold baked chicken and potato salad for dinner. We were halfway through eating when Maud said, "The phone must be out of order. Nobody's called Wilma." She picked up the receiver. "There's a dial tone. What's the problem, Wilma?" She hung up and the phone rang.

"Give it to me, Maud," Mom said.

"If it's Jared, I have to talk to him."

Maud gave Mom the phone.

"Hello." Pause. "I'm sorry. We're in the middle of dinner, Jared."

"Mom! Please!"

"Can she call you back?" Mom nodded. "All right." She hung up.

"What did he say?"

"You can call him after dinner."

I stood up. "I'm done."

She didn't let me get away with that. And after we finished eating, I had to help Maud clean up. Then I called him. I took the phone into my closet so Maud wouldn't hear.

"Where were you?" I said when he came on. "I looked for you after graduation."

"Brad was graduating from Elliot. We had to get over there. Wilma . . ."

Here we go. "What?" My mouth was dry.

"Are you okay?"

"Yeah." So far, so good.

"Something strange happened. I went to the library this afternoon to get books to read at camp. I had a huge stack in my arms. I was taking them to be checked out when I thought of you and dropped them all."

I forced myself to laugh. "Heavy thoughts. The books didn't land on your feet, did—"

"It was more than thinking about you. I can't describe it. I thought about you, and something was wrong. Something had changed, something had happened."

What did he mean? What did he think of me now?

"Then the feeling went away. Like it had come from somewhere else, not from inside me. I tried to call you, but people were using the phones at the library, and outside I couldn't find one that worked, and I had to—"

"I'm okay," I said. I tried to change the subject. "Ardis and—"

"That's not all. I ran into Ovideo. He lives down the block from me. And Timothy was with him—"

I swallowed. "And they thought about me too, at the same time as you. Right?"

"You know about it?"

"Sort of. What did they say?"

"How do you know?"

"It's a long story. What did they say?"

"Well, they weren't—uh, um—they weren't—uh—complimentary. They both said they didn't see why everyone was so crazy about you lately. I said I saw why."

"You did?"

"I said you only had to look at the caricature . . ."

The caricature! He had to remind them?

"What's going on, Wilma? Why did we all think of you at the same time?"

I had to tell him something. My heart was pounding. I didn't know if I could do this, if I could tell him. But I couldn't do it on the phone for sure. I had to be able to see how he was taking it, if he believed me, what he thought.

"Wilma?"

"I was thinking. I can't talk about it over the phone."

"A mystery. Spies on the airwaves." I could hear him smiling. Something about his voice had changed, and now he was smiling. Then he said he'd be downstairs when I took Reggie for his morning walk.

☼ ☼ ☼

The next morning, it took me forty-five minutes to get ready to walk Reggie. Without the spell, I had to look good. My zipper-neck T-shirt had a small stain on the shoulder. I wore it anyway after I tried on every other one I had. It was my favorite, and I'd worn it to the zoo.

Jared was waiting when I got downstairs.

"You have to kiss me," he said as soon as he saw me.

He didn't need answers first. He didn't need to check me out. I tied Reggie to the pole of a no-parking sign, and we kissed, a long one.

When it was over, I asked, "Why did I have to kiss you?"

"Because it's Sixty-sixth Street. We may be breaking the Rule by not kissing *continuously* on Sixty-sixth Street."

We walked toward the park. He took my hand and didn't say anything else. Maybe I wouldn't have to tell him. But after we crossed Broadway, he said, "The mystery. On the phone you wouldn't tell me what happened yesterday."

I chewed my lip.

"You look different today, too." He stood away from me, still holding my hand.

"Don't." I waved my free hand in front of my face. I didn't want him to evaluate me too, like Ardis and Nina and BeeBee had.

"You look good. Better, maybe. I give up." We took a few steps. Reggie sniffed a hydrant. "What happened?"

I thought of just saying that we'd been at my house fooling around with New Age spells, but then I remembered how tricked Ardis had felt. I didn't want to trick Jared anymore. I didn't want to trick anyone.

"It's going to sound completely weird . . ." I started.

"Not any weirder than what happened to me."

"Weirder. You'll see." I made myself start. "There was a witch in my kitchen yesterday afternoon."

Jared nodded. "Weirder."

"But that wasn't the first time I met her."

"No?"

"Don't laugh or I won't be able to tell it. She's very old."

"Naturally. She's a witch. Listen, Wilma, if you don't want to tell me—"

"I *don't* want to tell you. But I *am* telling you." We followed the path to Sheep Meadow. I dropped Reggie's leash, and he ran ahead. "Listen. It happened to Ardis and Nina and BeeBee and Daphne too. They were all at my house."

"Did they see the witch?"

"No. But they know it happened. I told them why, and they believe me. If you talk to them, they'll tell you. And if you call everybody who graduated yesterday, I bet they all thought of me at exactly the same second."

He was quiet. "All right. I'm a poet, or I want to be one. I should believe you."

"The first time I saw the old lady—or fairy or witch, whatever she is—the first time was . . ." And I told him about giving her a seat on the train. When I got to the part about the wish, he said, "What did you ask for? I know what I would have wanted."

"What?"

"Better poems. What did you ask for?"

He was going to think I was an idiot. "I asked her to make me the most popular kid at Claverford. And it ended yesterday because we graduated."

He didn't say anything for a minute. Then he said, "I didn't think popularity mattered to you." He stopped talking again.

I called Reggie, to give myself something to do.

What was he thinking? Was he angry, like Nina and Ardis had been?

He grinned. "You're great. I have to tell Brad about this. You cared that much about being popular and you still let Antoinette do the caricature. And you let me hang it in my locker." He told Reggie to sit. Reggie did, looking surprised. Then Jared kissed me again. And again. "You're even better than I thought."

I felt dizzy. I felt more turned upside down than when the spell began or ended. Jared didn't think I'd done anything terrible. He didn't feel tricked, maybe because he'd liked me before the spell started. If I wanted to be popular, and I made it my wish, there was nothing wrong with it.

It was really stupid, but in a second I was going to be crying my head off. I went to Reggie and touched my chest. He jumped up and licked my face. If my cheeks were wet, his tongue would be my excuse.

Jared started laughing. "But you missed your chance, Wilma. You could have gotten a pet elephant, or your own porpoise."

I could have. I never thought of it.

Epilogue

Jared said he'd call me from camp. I told him he should write too and send me more poems.

At Sixty-sixth Street and Broadway, he went down into the subway after such a long final kiss that Reggie started growling.

When I couldn't see him anymore, I walked Reggie a little longer. I wanted to be alone for a few minutes before I went home. At Sixty-fifth Street four or five people were waiting for the crosstown bus. I was almost past them when I saw her. The old lady. Waiting for the bus. My heart stopped. Why was she here?

I made Reggie heel and went up to her. She was facing down the street, looking for a bus. She didn't seem to notice me. "Excuse me." I didn't know her name.

She shuffled to face me. "Wilma! What a lovely surprise. I didn't expect to see you here."

Yeah. Right.

She smiled. "Congratulations. I see you're on your way to becoming a cool cat."

She could make sure I did, by giving me back my wish, by making it last as long as I wanted it to.

"What are you doing here?" I said.

"Why, I'm waiting for the bus. I just missed one."

"Can you . . . Would you . . ."

I heard Ardis's voice in my mind, as loud as if she were right next to me. "You'd do it again! You'd force us again. You don't get it."

Then I thought about Ovideo and Timothy, gossiping about me, saying mean things. When I went to Elliot in the fall, I'd have to put up with a lot of that from the kids who'd gone to Claverford.

I thought about Ardis and Nina and BeeBee, judging me, trying to make up their minds about being friends with me. I thought about them leaving yesterday still not positive, even though they were leaning in my direction.

The old lady could make it all better. She could make me exempt. I could judge everybody else, pick who I wanted, and never be judged.

And then I remembered wondering if Ardis and the rest of them really liked me, under the spell. I wanted friends who liked me *because* I was Wilma, *because* I had a caricature done, *because* I loved dogs and could imagine being one, *because* I helped an unpopular kid when Suzanne teased her. I wanted friends who liked me without a spell.

Maybe I could get a different wish, though. Maybe I could get her to give me a porpoise or an elephant, like Jared said. Or maybe she could change Maud into a chimpanzee. I'd love to share a room with a chimp.

"Could I do something else for you? Help you onto the bus? Pay your fare?" Stir your cauldron.

She chuckled. "That wouldn't be a good deed. You'd have an ulterior motive. You'd be doing it for yourself, not for me."

I noticed that she had perfect teeth, and her wrinkles seemed to be millions of laugh lines, so she always looked a little smiley. But who knew if this was her real shape. Her real shape could have thirteen legs and pincers and teeth like nails.

I might never see her again, and I wanted to know. "Is this your real shape?"

"What? My real shape? Oh. Yes, it certainly is."

"Oh. Well, isn't there anything I can do? I do other good deeds, help kids study, give to—"

"I'm sure you do, dear. I'm sure you're very sweet. But you can't do any more good deeds for me. And it's

probably not wise to turn your sister into a chimpanzee."
She smiled again. "Good-bye, Wilma." She shuffled to
look up the street again.

I couldn't force her to give me another wish. If I
tried, she could turn me into a toad. Besides, I had
Reggie. I didn't need a chimp. And—maybe—I had a
few friends. And Jared.

I started to walk away, but then I turned back and
went to one of the other people waiting for the bus, a boy
about my age. The old lady was still looking down the
street, away from us.

"When the bus comes," I whispered to the boy,
"help that old lady on. It's a good idea. You'll see."